A Bride For Seamus

By Linda Shenton Matchett

A Bride for Seamus
By Linda Shenton Matchett

Cover Design and author photo by: V. McKevitt

ISBN-13: 978-1-7347085-9-2

Published by Shortwave Press

Chapter One

White-hot shards of pain shot up Seamus Fitzpatrick's back, and he sucked in his breath, fighting the dizziness that threatened to topple him facedown into the dirt. With one hand on the horse's bridle, he bent over and whipped his handkerchief out of his pocket. Blotting at the perspiration streaming down his face, he waited for his vision to quit swimming.

The midday sun heated his shoulders under his cotton shirt while, Bess, the mare he'd purchased a couple of weeks ago, stood patiently by his side, seeming content to take a break from plowing. Seamus's head cleared, and he eased himself into an upright position. The muscles along his spine ached with a dull throb, but the piercing agony was gone. He blew out a deep breath and took a tentative step forward. Good. The ache was manageable. Doc Abbott had warned him the bullet that remained lodged in his body might never work its way out, and he'd suffer these episodes the rest of his life.

He'd prayed often for God to take care of the problem, but apparently He had other plans, and like the Apostle Paul, Seamus was destined to bear a constant thorn of the flesh. He wasn't enough of a Bible student to know if Paul's thorn was a physical ailment, but the man's writings were a balm on the worst days. Especially when his brother had an episode or his niece and nephew were cantankerous.

Bess nickered, then snorted and bobbed her head.

"Sorry, girl. I'm woolgathering. Sure, and we've got too many acres to prepare for planting for me to be turning my attention elsewhere." A hawk swooped in the cloudless sky overhead. A gorgeous day for sitting on the porch and putting up his feet. As if that were even possible. Numerous responsibilities awaited him inside as well, but with any luck the mail-order bride who'd arrived on last Saturday's train was doing something other than complaining.

He frowned and stuffed his handkerchief into his pocket. The third prospect in nine months, she'd responded to his ad in one of the eastern papers. After exchanging a handful of letters, he proposed she come to Iowa and meet him and the family before deciding if she wanted to marry. He'd been candid about the state of affairs, since the first two brides had informed him they never would have agreed to consider marrying him if they'd known about his brother. But in the few days since Julia Caron arrived, she'd caused dissension between the kids, frightened his brother on more than one occasion, and criticized the house and its contents. Her beauty appeared to be only skin deep. She cooked well enough, and her skills with a needle were exemplary, but those didn't make up for the spirit of unrest she'd brought with her.

A shriek sounded from the house, then shouting, and Seamus's gaze shot in that direction. Julia and Conor stormed out of the house. She pointed her finger in his brother's face, her lips curled in a sneer. He couldn't hear her words, but her attitude was clear enough from her expression. Something had happened between the two of them. Again.

Conor's face looked mulish, but he didn't respond, just stood in the yard with his arms crossed and his head shaking back and forth like a bull presented with a red cape. The woman finished her tirade, then marched back inside, slamming the door.

"Something's got to change, Bess." Seamus unhooked the mare from the plow and swung up onto her back. He turned her toward the house and gave her sides a gentle squeeze with his knees. With a whinny, she broke into a trot. "I know. Not what you had planned. Me neither."

He stopped the horse in the yard, slid from her back, and wrapped the reins over the porch railing. "Conor, what's going on?"

"I didn't do nuthin'." Conor scowled and headed to the barn.

"That's not what I asked...oh, never mind." Seamus stepped onto the porch and reached for the knob but missed as the door was flung open from inside.

Satchel in hand, Julia glowered at him. "I'm leaving. I've had enough. You'd better get used to being single, Mr. Fitzpatrick, because no woman in her right mind is going to take on this family. Your brother needs to be in an institution, and the children need a firm hand. You are too lenient with them, and they balk at any sort of discipline. I believe there is a three o'clock train, and I'd like to be on it."

"Miss Caron—"

"I've made up my mind, so don't ask me to stay." She looked down her nose at him, her lips nearly disappearing.

"I'm not. I was going to apologize that this...uh, arrangement didn't work out, and I'll hook Bess to the wagon as soon as I wash up."

"Oh." Her face reddened, and she had the decency to look abashed.

"Or I'd be happy to put you up in the hotel in town if you want to stay and try to find yourself another groom."

"No, thank you. I'd like to go home, if you please."

"Yes, ma'am." He took the bag from her and gestured to the rocking chair. "Why don't you have a seat, and I'll be ready in a jiffy."

She lowered herself in the chair and wrapped her arms around her middle, staring into the distance.

He studied her for a long moment, then descended the stairs and grabbed Bess's halter. He led her to the barn and hooked her to buckboard while his brother mucked one of the stalls. Conor must be fired up. He rarely took the initiative to clean out the barn. "She's leaving. I'll be back in a couple of hours. Will you be okay while I'm gone?"

"Yeah." Conor leaned on the shovel. "This is my fault, isn't it?"

"No. She's not a fit for lots of reasons." He clapped his brother on the shoulder. "God will send someone, Conor. You'll see."

"If you say so."

Seamus stifled a sigh. He wasn't convinced, but Conor didn't deserve to feel bad for the woman's departure. He climbed onto the wagon and drove it to the front of the house. Minutes later he was back on board having loaded her bag and trunk and taken a quick sponge bath. The ride to the station seemed interminable, but they managed to get there without incident. He paid for her ticket and gave her additional cash to assuage his guilt over the relief of seeing her go. Would God truly send someone, or was he kidding himself to believe there was a woman somewhere who would love their family such as it was?

Chapter Two

Dust motes flew into the air, dancing in the sunlight glaring through the bedroom curtains. Madeline Winthrop coughed and waved her hand in front of her face. Cleaning house had been on the bottom of the list while caring for Father during his last days, but she hadn't realized how bad things had gotten until now. Her face heated as she wrapped the crystal vase from her dresser and tucked it into the trunk. She wouldn't have much use for such a frivolous item, but she refused to leave any personal effects behind.

"Are you all right, Madeline?" Her younger sister, Cecilia, entered the room, her honey-blonde hair swept into a flawless pile of ringlets. Even in a simple cotton dress, her youngest sister managed to look regal.

"Fine. Almost finished packing." Madeline smoothed her skirts, then tucked the lock of hair behind her ear that had pulled free from the bun at the base of her head. Straight and heavy, her auburn hair never behaved well enough to be worn in fashionable styles. Not that she needed to worry about society's expectations anymore. Her sisters had made good matches, but at her age with plain looks, and lack of a dowry, no one would be vying for her hand.

She blew out a deep breath, went to her nightstand, and pulled out her diary and Bible. She laid them in the open trunk, then cast her gaze around the room. Every surface was cleared and her bed stripped of its linens, giving the vast space a forlorn look.

Footsteps sounded in the hall, and her middle sister, Phoebe, appeared in the doorway, her thickened waistline straining at her dress. She carried the family Bible, large and bulky. Perspiration shone on her forehead, and her voice was breathless, probably from taking the two flights of stairs to the bedroom level of the house. "Do want to take this with you?"

"No, you keep it, so you can show your children." Madeline shook her head, and her heart tugged. "Tell them about their grandparents." Her hands fumbled in the pocket of her skirt, and she pulled out a mahogany pipe, the woodsy scent of her father's favorite tobacco filling her nose. She caressed the polished bowl, then placed the memento next to the cloth-wrapped vase. At least she had something from each of her parents. She straightened her spine and brushed her hands together. She must be strong for her sisters. "That's the last of it. I still have a week before I need to vacate, giving me plenty of time to make lodging arrangements."

Cecilia's brow furrowed. "Why not stay and take Uzziah up on his offer to marry you? He's older, but still handsome."

Madeline shuddered. Marry her father's partner? Not if he were the last man on earth. His eyes seemed to undress her whenever he looked at her, and his oily smile held secrets she could only imagine. No, poverty was a more palatable alternative.

"I'm sorry Father didn't leave you the house, Maddie." Tears shimmered in Phoebe's hazel eyes. "It's not fair. The law says he could have bequeathed the property to you."

"Yes, but he chose not to. He probably thought I would be married and taken care of at the time he made his will." Madeline sighed. "He hid his illness from all of us. By the time we realized what was happening, it was too late. The damage was done to his mind, and no attorney would execute any documents under his signature."

"You should take Uzziah to court." Cecilia stood among the trunks and boxes, her fisted hands on her hips. "A judge might rule in your favor."

Phoebe gasped. "Drag our family name through the newspapers with a lawsuit? Shame on you, Cecilia."

"You care more about reputation than your own sister?" Cecilia glowered and crossed her arms.

"Stop." Madeline held up her hands. "I've already discussed the situation with an attorney. He feels my chances of success are slim at best, so I will not be seeking restitution."

"But what will you do? How will you survive if you won't live with either of us?"

"I'm perfectly capable of taking care of myself. I've got a good education. Perhaps I could seek a position as a governess or a teacher at one of the boarding schools."

"You would *work*?" Phoebe's lips twisted as if she'd eaten a lemon.

"Work is not a dirty word, Phoebe, and I've prayed about my circumstances. God will provide some sort of solution. I must trust Him."

"But He only has a few days."

Madeline chuckled, then checked the watch pinned to her bodice. "True. Be that as it may, I'm sure something will work out. As a matter of fact, I must leave to go visit Pastor Nelson to pick up his letter of reference. Perhaps he will have a recommendation."

"Would you like us to go with you?" Cecilia cocked her head. "Afterward, we could go to the bookstore. You love books."

"No, you girls run along. You've got husbands to attend and households to run. I'll be fine." Madeline hugged her sisters, then grabbed her blue wool cloak from the closet. "Let's do tea the day after tomorrow. How does that sound?"

They nodded and followed her down the stairs and out of the house. She locked the door and tucked the key into her reticule. Giving her sisters one more hug, she turned south, listening to their fading footsteps. She swallowed the lump in her throat as she hurried down the sidewalk. She'd put on a brave face for Phoebe and Cecilia, but truth be told, she was clinging to her faith by a thread.

Minutes later, she arrived at the sandstone church. She trudged up the steps and entered the dim sanctuary. Sunlight glittered through the stained-glass windows casting rainbows of color across the pews. The pastor stood near the altar speaking in hushed tones to an elderly man. They shook hands, and the man strode down the aisle, nodding to her as he passed.

"Miss Winthrop." Pastor Nelson approached, a wide smile on his face. "So glad you could make it." He gestured toward the nearest pew, and they sat on the hard benches. He withdrew an envelope from his breast pocket. "Here is the reference I promised, but you may not need it."

Her heart skipped a beat. Had he found a position for her already? What would she be doing? She took the letter and tucked it in her bag, then laced her fingers to keep them from shaking. She nodded, not trusting herself to speak.

"I've heard from a friend of mine out West, Iowa to be exact. He's also a pastor, and one of his congregants is looking for a wife. His brother is not well and has two children. The man has been taking care of all of them and trying to run his farm. He needs help, and he wants more than a housekeeper. He's been unsuccessful using the mail-order-bride system."

She narrowed her eyes, and her skin crawled. "Why? What aren't you telling me?"

Pastor Nelson cleared his throat. "The man's name is Seamus Fitzpatrick, and—"

"Irish?" Madeline's lip curled.

"Just because your parents disdained the Irish doesn't make it right." He looked over his spectacles at her. "According to my friend, Seamus is a decent, hardworking, and God-fearing man. The reason the brides have not stayed is his brother. He was in the war, and he came home...damaged. He can barely see to his own needs, let alone those of his children."

"But I'm not a nurse."

"No, you're not, but his brother's problems aren't physical."

"His mind. He lost his mind in the war."

He blew out a deep breath and slumped against the pew. "Yes. I thought with your experience in caring for your father, this would be an answer to a prayer for you and Mr. Fitzpatrick."

Marriage. To someone she'd never met. To an Irishman. "I don't know, Pastor." She nibbled on her lower lip.

"I understand your hesitancy." He patted her hand. "There is one more thing. Should you decide to go through with this, you would need to marry by proxy before you go."

"Proxy?"

"Someone would stand in for Mr. Fitzpatrick, and I would marry the two of you."

"And if we were married, I'd be bound to stay. He must be quite desperate." She plucked at her skirt, mind racing. "Can I think about the offer?"

"Two days. That's all I can give you."

"I'll get back to you before then." She rose and hurried out the door. Was this the answer God was providing? Had caring for her father been in preparation for helping this man's brother? Could she move to the wilds of Iowa and marry an Irishman?

Moments later, she was inside the house. As she removed her hat and hung her cloak on the stand in the entryway, a knock sounded. She opened the door and cringed.

Dressed in a hand-tailored suit and crisply pressed white shirt, Uzziah stood on the porch. He dipped his head in greeting. "May I come in, Miss Winthrop?"

"No, I'm sorry. I'm quite busy." She pasted a smile on her face. "Perhaps if you had called ahead, I could have rearranged my day."

"Perhaps if *you* hadn't been galivanting around the city, you would have time to see me."

Her eyebrow shot up, and she hid her clenched hands in the folds of her skirt. "What I choose to do with my time is none of your affair. I bid you good day, sir." She started to close the door.

He blocked it with his foot and leaned through the gap. "Don't cross me, Miss Winthrop. I have connections all over this city. If you hope to provide for yourself, you'd be well-served to treat me with respect." He put his fingers to the brim of his hat in a mock salute, then turned and swaggered down the steps.

With trembling hands, she closed the door, then leaned her forehead against the wood, its painted surface cool under her skin.

Rapping sounded, and her heart leapt into her throat. She yanked open the door. “I told you...oh...Pastor Nelson.” Her faced heated, and she moved aside. “Would you like to come in?”

Holding up her lace-edged handkerchief, he shook his head. “I’m not here to stay. You must have dropped this during our conversation.”

“Thank you.” She took the hanky and stuffed it into her pocket. “Pastor, I’d be happy to marry Mr. Fitzpatrick. Is tomorrow too soon?”

Chapter Three

The train rocked and bumped as it hurtled along the tracks. Madeline hunched into her seat clutching her satchel and stared out the window. The scenery had changed numerous times in the four days since she'd boarded. She rotated her neck to ease the stiffness in her back. Only a an hour remained until she arrived in Cedar Rapids. Her pulse skittered. The marriage ceremony in the pastor's office had been short and to the point with Cecilia's husband Horace standing in for her groom.

Of the family, he'd been the only one to commend her on finding a solution to her problem. He'd been gracious and warm, easing some of the nervousness that had assailed her when she'd entered the church. Phoebe and Cecilia had watched the proceedings with pursed lips, then given her a cursory hug at the end.

Seamus had wired enough money; she could afford to stay in a hotel, so she'd shed a few tears as she stood in her bedroom for the last time, then vacated the house without a backward glance. Fortunately, as far as she knew, Uzziah was none the wiser as to where she'd gone, so he was no longer of any concern.

Pastor Nelson had made arrangements for her luggage to be taken to the train station, then accompanied her in the hansom cab. He'd prayed over her and promised to write. Her sisters hadn't made the same commitment. Was her decision so distasteful they would sever their relationship? She sniffled and blinked back tears.

"Are you all right, miss?" The young woman who'd boarded at the last stop and sat next to Madeline patted her arm. "Is there anything I can do for you?"

Madeline's face warmed. Her sisters would be appalled that she'd been caught upset in public. She shrugged. "Just missing my family."

"'Tis understandable. Are you traveling far?"

"Iowa."

"My, that is a fair distance, isn't it?" She smiled. "I'm going there myself as a mail-order bride. Des Moines." Her face shone. "Been writing the man I'll be marrying for several months. I cannot wait to see him. Are you also a mail-order bride?"

"I'm not sure what I am. I don't know my husband, and we were married by proxy before I left Boston."

"Well, isn't that something?" The woman extended her hand. "By the way, my name is Elspeth. I should have introduced myself when I first sat down, but it's all been a bit overwhelming. 'Tis the first time I've ridden this far on a train, and I've been sitting here wondering what it will be like to live in the country." Elspeth's cheeks pinked. "And I hope he likes what he sees. We agreed not to exchange photographs."

"You don't know what your fiancé looks like?"

"No, but I already love him. His letters have shown me who he is on the inside: a caring, intelligent man who loves the Lord. I couldn't ask for a better husband."

"I'm happy for you."

"If I may be so bold, you must have been desperate to marry a man you've neither met nor corresponded with."

"My circumstances were dire, but he comes recommended by a friend of my pastor who is also a man of the cloth. So, I'm hopeful my husband is a trustworthy and decent man as described."

Elspeth pressed her hands to her chest, eyes glowing. "You are very brave, and this is the most romantic thing I've ever heard. He's rescuing you as a knight in shining armor."

Was he liberating her, or would she be trapped in another difficult situation?

The train slowed, brakes squealing, and she peeked out the window. In the distance, buildings appeared on the horizon. Her palms slicked with sweat, and her breath hitched. Was this how a deer felt when caught in the sight of a hunter? She was being foolish. She made her choice, and in the safety of Pastor Nelson's office, considered it a good one. Why second-guess herself now?

Steam enveloped the car as the train chugged into the station. Elspeth rose, and Madeline gathered her satchel and moved into the aisle.

The young woman wrapped her in a quick embrace. "I'll be praying that your marriage is successful."

"Thank you, and I'll do the same for you."

Heart thumping in her chest, Madeline followed the departing passengers and climbed down the steps. Laughter, shouts, and conversations filled the air. Trunks thudded as they were removed from the baggage cars and piled on the platform. Her gaze ricocheted around the chaos. Several men eyed her, but no one came forward to ask her identity. Had she misread the telegram containing instructions?

She fumbled into her bag and pulled out the paper, then scanned the words. No misunderstanding. He'd indicated he would be waiting for her upon her arrival. Minutes passed. The train pulled away, and soon she was alone. Where was her new husband? A chill swept over her. Had he changed his mind?

Lips trembling, she hurried inside the squatty station and went to the window. "I'm Madeline Winthrop, er, Fitzpatrick. Any message for me?"

"No, ma'am."

"Thank you." Tears threatened. Her stomach rumbled, and she turned back to the window. "Is there somewhere I may get something to eat?"

"Yes, ma'am. Head out of the—"

"Miss Winthrop?"

Madeline whirled and came face-to-face with a man about her height with dark blonde hair and eyes the color of her mother's peridot ring. Dust marred his face, and his clothes were rumpled and dirty. "Yes?"

"I'm Seamus Fitzpatrick. Please accept my apology for being late." He shuffled his feet and looked past her. "Do you have luggage?"

Could her husband have at least bathed before coming to meet her for the first time? "Yes, on the platform. It will be easy to find."

Understanding dawned in his eyes, and he flushed. "Because it's the only baggage there?"

"Yes." What had she gotten herself into?

##

Seamus stiffened, and the muscle in his jaw jumped. "I'll explain on the way home. My intention was not to greet you thirty minutes late wearing filthy clothes. But you'll find that our lives don't always go as planned." He gestured toward the doorway. "I'll put you in the wagon, then return for your bags."

Her face pinked, and she ducked her head. "Thank you."

He led her outside, his lips pressed together. With any luck it was fatigue from the journey that made her snippy and shrewish rather than entrenched personality traits like his last potential mate.

She stopped next to the buckboard and gave it a dubious stare. "How do I get inside?"

"You've never ridden in a wagon?"

"No, I haven't the faintest idea how to climb on board."

"It's easy. I'll help you." He pointed to the wheel. "You put your foot there, then you'll be able to step inside." He gripped her hand, and his eyes widened as tingles shot up his arm.

She did as he directed and sat down with a triumphant smile. "That wasn't so hard."

"You did well. I'll be right back." He trotted through the building and lifted her trunk. Lighter than expected. Was she shipping additional items, or did she plan to skedaddle if things were too difficult? He huffed out a breath. Time would tell, but was the clock running out? He put the chest in the wagon and returned for the small crate. Finally ensconced in the buckboard, he slapped the reins, and they began the journey home.

They rode in silence for several minutes, her slender form rigid beside him. The steady clip-clop of the horse's hooves soothed his jangled nerves. He should make conversation, but where to start?

"I wanted to—"

"How far—"

He gave her a sidelong glance. "You first."

"I wondered how far your homestead is from town."

"About eight miles. We should be there in a little over an hour."

She nodded. "The scenery is quite beautiful. So...expansive."

"Not like the city where you're from."

"No."

Seamus cleared his throat. "Listen. About being late and all. We had an incident with my brother. Sometimes he has...uh...episodes when he thinks he's back in the war. He becomes frightened. This time he disappeared. We had to find him. I knew you would be safe at the train station, but anything could have happened to Conor. Especially if we didn't find him before dark. I'm sorry I was unable to get word to you."

"I understand." The tone of her voice contradicted her words.

His grip tightened on the reins. "Why don't we try to get to know each other a bit? Perhaps that will set you more at ease." He sent her what he hoped was a reassuring smile. "I could start, and you can ask as many questions as you like. How does that sound?"

"Okay."

The right-hand wagon wheels rolled through a deep hole he should have remembered, and she fell against him, her hand clutching his thigh. Mouth gaping, she pulled back as if scalded. Her face was red to the roots of her thick auburn hair, the color of roasted chestnuts. His leg thrummed from the feel of her palm. How could she create a physical response in their short time together?

"I'm sorry. I forgot about the dip in the road. It won't happen again."

"Is it difficult to drive a wagon?" Her eyes were clouded, and she seemed to be studying the harness.

"No, it just takes practice. Would you like to try?"

"Maybe another day, but thank you for the offer."

"You will need to learn. Any good farmwife can drive."

"I hope you won't be disappointed."

Was that trepidation in her voice? Her emotions changed direction faster than a runaway herd of cattle. What would it be like to live with her day after day? How would she behave with Conor? Had he made the biggest mistake of his life agreeing to this arrangement?

Chapter Four

The wagon rolled to a stop in front of the house, and Madeline narrowed her gaze. She hadn't expected a mansion, but to use the term rustic was generous. The home was little more than a shanty, with the barn being three times its size. The animals lived better than it appeared she would. A small porch sagged, several of its railing posts missing. The door was a handful of planks nailed together, and all but one of the window panes were greased paper rather than glass. There wasn't a flower garden in sight.

She realized she was gaping and clamped her jaw. During the remainder of the ride, Seamus had explained that most of his time was spent with farm chores and care for his brother. He did the best he could with the kids, but they were often on their own. Schooling them was intermittent and mostly consisted of reading from the Bible and doing simple ciphering. Driving them into town was not practical.

He'd also told her about her predecessors. Three of them to be exact. The most recent had fled the premises a month ago. None of them had stayed very long. Nor had done anything with the house. She had her work cut out for her.

Seamus climbed out of the wagon and came around to her side. He held up his arms, and she grasped his shoulders as he lifted her to the ground. His large hands were firm and sure around her waist, and her face heated at his touch. He released her, then gestured toward the house. "You'll be sleeping in my room, and I'll be in the barn until we're...uh...comfortable with each other. Conor will be in the barn, too."

They walked inside, and she stifled a gasp. The sink was stacked with soiled dishes, and more sat on the table. Dirt covered the wooden floor, and a trail of footprints created a path around the room. Fortunately, there was a small stove, and she wouldn't be required to cook on an open fire. Tattered curtains hung over the windows.

"I'd planned to have this cleaned and ready, but..." His words died, and he rubbed the back of his neck, his gaze downcast.

Her heart tugged. He seemed to be making an effort, and at least realized this was an unacceptable way to live. "I'm used to hard work, Mr. Fitzpatrick. I can take care of this in a jiffy."

"Would you like to lie down or freshen up? I'll bring in your things, then wash up outside. One of the neighbors brought lunch and dinner that we can eat cold or reheat depending on your preference."

Madeline shook her head. She wouldn't tell him she couldn't sleep with the house in such poor condition. "Thank you, but I dozed on the train. I'll set things to rights in here, then I'll be ready to clean up and change my clothes. Would you show me the barn and the rest of the property?"

"I'm glad you want to see the place." He beamed. "And you can meet Conor, too. The kids are with the same neighbor who brought the food. They'll be away for a couple of days, until you get settled in a bit."

"You've thought of everything, haven't you?"

"Probably not, but I want you to feel welcome...at home here." He tugged at his collar. "I want our marriage to be successful."

"Me, too." Her knees quaked.

Moments later, he'd set her luggage in the bedroom, a small and inviting room, then headed outside. The bed was covered with a blue-and-yellow, nine-patch quilt and flanked by a pair of pine nightstands. A mirror hung above a matching pine dresser that held a pitcher and basin. A ladder-back chair stood in one corner, and a watercolor painting was tacked the wall to the left of the door. Was her husband an artist? Despite their conversation in the wagon, she knew little about the man.

With a last glance at the bed, which beckoned, she left the room and surveyed the living area. She could do this. She would do this. There was no alternative. Straightening her spine, she marched to the table and scraped the food into the trash bin, then filled the sink with water and submerged the dishes to let them soak. She filled the kettle and lit the stove so she could use hot water to wash the items.

She collected what appeared to be the twins' schoolbooks and papers and piled them on the table near the rocking chair. She rummaged until she found a broom and swept the dirt out the front door. She'd scrub the floor later. Perspiration trickled between her shoulder blades and down the sides of her face, but she smiled in satisfaction. The house looked better already. As Madeline finished the dishes, the door opened behind her, and she turned. Seamus and a man, whose resemblance was so strong to her husband that he could only be her brother-in-law, stood on the threshold. Her mouth dried, and her pulse tripped. She'd been so put out at Seamus's tardiness, she'd missed how handsome he was.

Hair still damp and clinging to his collar, Seamus had changed into a fresh shirt that stretched across his broad chest and was tucked in at the waist. His green eyes sparkled against his tanned skin. A wide smile lit his face. "Sure, and you've been busy. The place looks wonderful. I'm grateful for the time you took cleaning after your arduous journey."

Her stomach buzzed as if a swarm of bees had taken flight. "It was nothing. Just a little elbow grease."

"Nonsense. You shouldn't have had to set things right before unpacking."

"It couldn't be helped." She laid down the towel and walked toward the stranger, arm outstretched. "You must be Conor. I'm Madeline. It's a pleasure to meet you."

Tall and gangly, Conor had jet-black hair and ice-blue eyes that studied her with wariness. He made no move to shake her hand, so she dropped it to her side.

She cleared her throat and gestured toward the table where she'd put plates, silverware, and napkins. "If you'll sit, I can set out dinner."

Seamus shook his head. "No, for the rest of the evening I'll wait on you. You've already done more than enough." He walked to the table and held out a chair, an expectant expression softening his gaze.

"All right. Thank you." Her heart hammered in her chest. What was wrong with her? A bit of cordialness, and she was swooning like a schoolgirl with her first crush. As he pushed in her chair, she smelled his fresh scent of soap. She stifled the urge to take a deep breath.

Conor dropped into the chair across the table, and Seamus strode to the stove and retrieved the food. He put down platters and bowls, then poured water into their glasses from a pitcher. Sitting on the end of the table to her left, he reached for her hand and Conor's. "I'll say the blessing."

Madeline clasped her cold fingers in his warm palm, and tingles zipped up her arm. She gasped, then clamped her lips together. Conor took Seamus's hand but didn't extend his arm to her. She sent him what she hoped was a reassuring smile but kept her right hand in her lap.

"Father, thank You for this day, and thank You for bringing Madeline to us safe and sound. Thank You for her willingness to join the family, and, er, help me to be a good husband. I ask that You help her feel at home with us. Help us to seek You in all that we do. Bless this food to our bodies, and bless those who provided it for us. In Jesus' name, amen." He winked and gave her hand a quick squeeze before releasing her fingers.

Her breath hitched, and she smiled. Perhaps things would work out after all.

"You've been days on a train, yet you've accomplished so much already. You must be ready to keel over."

"I'm tired, but after being cooped up with little to do but sit, activity felt good."

"Well, I'm grateful, and rest assured I'll do the dinner dishes. You should lie down afterward."

"I might sit on the porch for a bit, if you don't mind."

"And I'll join you once I've done my chores." A dimple appeared in his left cheek as he grinned.

"That would be nice." She glanced up and froze.

Conor glared at her, his mouth twisted in a deep frown. His eyes were clouded and distant. "Why are you here?"

"I beg your pardon?" Her lips felt stiff.

"Why did you come? We don't need you."

Seamus put his hand on his brother's arm. "Conor, Madeline is here because I asked her to come. She's my wife."

"Your wife? Your wife!" Conor slammed his hand on the table and jumped up, his chair falling onto the floor with a bang. "You never said anything about getting married." Fists on his hips, he shook his head back and forth. "Never."

Eyes wide, she watched as Seamus got up and put his arm around his brother's shoulders and led him to the couch. He murmured in Conor's ear, and his brother's agitation seemed to ebb a bit. They sat down, and Seamus continued to talk. She couldn't hear what he said, but the timbre of his voice was low and soothing. Madeline nibbled on her lower lip. Had Seamus not told his brother, or was forgetfulness part of his mental problems? Pastor Nelson hadn't been specific about the man's infirmities.

Sing, My child.

She stilled.

Sing for them.

The first song that came to mind was "Amazing Grace." Her mother sang the hymn to her and her sisters every night at bedtime. Tears pricked the backs of her eyes as Madeline began to sing, low at first, then with more confidence.

Seamus looked at her and nodded as Conor sighed and sagged against his brother.

Perhaps she was in the right place after all.

Chapter Five

Seamus dried the last plate and stacked it with the rest on the hutch. He hung the damp towel on a hook next to the window above the sink as Madeline wiped down the counters. She'd sung hymn after hymn, and despite Conor's initial agitation with her, he'd calmed at the sound of her melodious contralto voice. At one point, he'd joined her, but remained quiet for the most part. After about thirty minutes, he bade them good night and wandered out to the barn, giving the two of them time to clean up the dinner dishes.

She wiped her hands on the apron around her waist. "Thank you for helping with cleanup. I can't imagine my father ever performing kitchen chores."

"Your family had servants."

"True, but even if we lived simply, I can't see it."

He shrugged. "In the beginning after Conor's wife, Tillie, died, I had to take care of everything. He was in no state to help, then I found I enjoyed the solitude and satisfaction of putting everything to rights."

Her face pinked. "I didn't think about that aspect. Forgive me."

"Nothing to forgive." He studied her face, its porcelain skin clear and fair. Did she realize how attractive she was? "Your voice is beautiful. Have you had lessons?"

Her cheeks darkened, and she shook her head. “No. I can carry a tune, nothing more.”

“I beg to differ. I’ve never heard singing so clear and heartfelt. God has gifted you with a wonderful voice.”

“I do feel close to Him when I sing. I can sense Him smiling, but I never considered singing a gift, especially compared to one of the girls at church. She had an exquisite voice, operatic, I would say.”

“But your songs are worship, and that’s better than performing.” He gestured toward the bedroom door. “You must be exhausted. Would you like to go to retire for the night?”

“No. I don’t think I could sleep yet. I’ll sit by the fireplace for a bit. Perhaps that will relax me.”

“You’ve had an eventful day. You only just got off the train this morning.”

“Doesn’t seem possible.” Madeline removed her apron before draping it on the sink. Skirts rustling, she walked to the nearest chair, then lowered herself into the seat with a sigh. An errant strand of hair dangled beside her face, and he crossed his arms to prevent tucking the shining lock behind her ear. How was she still awake after all that had happened?

He sat beside her and stretched out his legs. Embers glowed, and an occasional flame licked at the charred logs. “This is my favorite part of the day. I usually read, but maybe I’ll have you sing to me from now on.”

“You’re teasing, aren’t you?” She cocked her head, a tentative smile on her lips.

"Only partially. You don't give yourself enough credit for how lovely you sound."

"What gifts do you have?"

Seamus shrugged. "None that I can think of."

"God gifts every one of us. There must be some special capability you have."

"The gift of farming?" He grinned. "The gift of washing dishes."

Madeline giggled and shook her head.

His chest swelled. How could she already be burrowing her way into his heart? He cleared his throat. "I'll give some thought to what my gifts are. Meanwhile, it's too dark for that tour I promised, but I can tell you about our place and Cedar Rapids."

"I'd like that. Cedar Rapids is larger than I expected."

"During the 1850s, a lot of Czechs emigrated to the U.S. because of revolutions in the Austrian empire and took advantage of the cheap land here in the West. Then Thomas Sinclair opened his meatpacking company, which created almost four hundred jobs. The Homestead Act brought a bunch of folks. My folks moved here in the early forties before Conor and I were born."

Her eyes widened. "This is your parents' home?"

"Yes, and no." He swallowed a lump that had formed in his throat. "There was a fire, and most of the house was destroyed. They didn't survive."

"Oh, Seamus, I'm so sorry." She squeezed his arm. "How awful. And then your sister-in-law's death, and Conor's problems. You've had a difficult time."

Warmth spread from her fingers through his shirt sleeve. "I didn't get to say goodbye. The fire occurred while I was away at war."

"How—"

"The neighbors say it must have been an accident. No battles occurred in Iowa, so it wasn't as if enemy troops set the house ablaze. I assumed I wasn't getting letters because of poor mail service and didn't find out until I came home and saw the burned-out structure."

"What a tragedy. Does Conor understand about your parents?"

"Yes. And their deaths added to the strain of what he experienced during the war. So much killing. Then to come home and find our parents dead and to lose Tillie during the twins' birth. I think that's why he's retreated into his mind. Life had dealt him too many blows."

"Why does God allow war?" Tears shimmered in Madeline's eyes.

"A question smarter people than me have been asking for millennia." He shook his head and held up the thick book on the table near his elbow. "I didn't mean to create a somber mood. How about if I read to us for a bit? Do you like Jules Verne? He's written extraordinary stories. I recently purchased *From the Earth to the Moon.*

"I've heard of him, but haven't had a chance to read any of his works. My recent favorite is Louisa May Alcott's *Little Women.* But I enjoy discovering new authors, so I look forward to hearing Mr. Verne's books."

Seamus smiled, turned to the first chapter, and began to read. He was soon engrossed in the story, imagining himself seated in the Baltimore Gun Club listening to Impey Barbicane pitch his idea of creating a cannon to shoot a projectile of some sort to the moon. Time passed, and he rubbed his burning eyes.

He glanced at Madeline whose eyes were closed and head lolled to one shoulder. How long had she been asleep? He'd been so absorbed in the story he'd forgotten her presence. What sort of husband forgets about his wife? He closed the book and laid it on the table, then rose. He gathered her in his arms and carried her to the bedroom.

Light as a feather, she mumbled and wrapped her arm around his neck, then nestled under his chin. His heart skittered, and he laid her on the mattress, removed her shoes, and covered her with the quilt. The moonlight shone through the window and cast a glow on her face. A faint smile curved her lips, and she sighed. Before he could change his mind, he bent and pressed a kiss on her forehead.

He studied her for a long moment, then slipped from the room, and closed the door. He doused the lights and headed out the door for the barn. What a complex woman. Strong-willed enough to flee her parents' attempts to marry her off yet gentle with his brother. Small in stature but strong enough to clean house after a four-day train ride. Beautiful on the outside as well as the inside. Could he be enough for her? Would she learn to care for him?

Chapter Six

Madeline opened her eyes and blinked. Sunlight streamed through the window across the bed. She yawned and looked down, realizing she still wore yesterday's dress. Her shoes sat side by side next to her open trunk. Her stomach hollowed. Seamus must have carried her into the bedroom. What must he think of her falling asleep as he read aloud? Her mother would horrified at her behavior, but what did her new husband think?

Her gaze shot to the space beside her, and she ran her hand over the smooth sheets. It didn't appear he'd joined her last night. He'd apparently slept in the barn as promised. Memories of his deep voice rumbling in his chest flood into her mind. A voice that changed inflection with description and dialogue as he brought the story alive. Her assumption of meeting an uncouth, uneducated farmer had been shattered. He was nothing like she'd anticipated. What other expectations would be crushed?

She swung her feet onto the small braided run and wiggled her toes. Her stomach gurgled, and she pressed her hand against her belly. She padded to the pitcher and basin on the dresser. He'd freshened the water and laid a chunk of soap on top of a clean towel. She stripped and gave herself a sponge bath, then brushed her hair and pinned it into a bun. Pinching her cheeks to give them color, she eyed herself in the tiny mirror and frowned. Her socialite days had ceased with her father's death, but the transformation to farmwife was disconcerting.

After lacing up her shoes, she made the bed and put away her clothes. She'd leave the trunk for him to handle. She wiped her damp hands on her skirts and opened the door. "Hello?" She walked into the living area. "Hello?" The cabin was empty. She went to the kitchen where a note lay on the table indicating her breakfast was warming in the oven, and Seamus was in the fields.

Of course he was. He didn't have time to wait on a wife who'd stayed in bed well past time for rising. She opened the oven and pulled out a plate filled with scrambled eggs, fried ham, a pair of biscuits, and several pancakes. Did he think her appetite so large, or had he provided a selection of food for her choosing? She sat down and put a napkin in her lap. Thoughts of Seamus's hand in hers as he asked the blessing brought heat to her face. She bowed her head. "Father, thank You for Seamus and the opportunity You've afforded us. Help me to be a good wife and not a disappointment to him. There's so much I have to learn. And be with me as I try to care for Conor. Give him a spirit of peace. Thank You for the food You've provided."

A blanket of warmth settled on her shoulders, and the tightness in her back eased as she picked up her fork and dug into the fragrant breakfast. The ham's saltiness mingled with the eggs' creaminess, and the flapjacks were light and fluffy. She'd never tasted food so delicious. Hunger satiated, she washed her plate and silverware before heading outside.

The aroma of freshly turned dirt clung to the breeze that stroked her cheeks. Sunlight glared, and she shielded her eyes as she surveyed the expanse. A hundred yards away, the men worked in the fields. Seamus rode some sort of conveyance led by a horse. A plow? She had so much to learn. Hopefully, her new husband was a patient man.

Madeline set off toward the men, and her heels sank into the soft earth. Clearly her shoes and most of her clothes would need to be replaced with more practical attire. She lifted her skirts and hurried in their direction. As she approached, she waved her hands.

Seamus reined in the horse, his face lighting up with a broad smile. He climbed down and shouted, "Conor, can you take over?"

His brother nodded, then trotted to the vehicle and hoisted himself onto the seat. He clicked his teeth and slapped the horse's rump with the leather straps. "Giddyup." The wheels lurched forward, and the steel blade carved a trench in the soil.

She cocked her head. "You're plowing, right?"

He chuckled and nodded. "Yes. I take it you've never seen a plow before."

"No. There aren't too many on the streets of Boston."

"Touché." He stuffed his hands into his pockets. "Did you find the food I left for you? How did you sleep?"

Her cheeks warmed. "Yes, breakfast was delicious. I'm sorry I didn't awaken until late. You've been out here for hours, haven't you?"

"Yes, but I didn't take a lengthy train ride, clean house, and calm a distraught man. You obviously needed your rest." He shuffled his feet. "What would you like to do today? I won't have time to give you the tour until later this afternoon when we've finished this plot."

"When are the children returning?"

"We have two more days until they'll be home, so you'll have plenty of time to familiarize yourself with the inside of the house and their schoolwork."

"If you don't need me out here, I'll finish cleaning inside."

"Things didn't go as planned yesterday, and you've not had a chance to bathe. I could have Conor bring the tub inside and fill it with water. Would you like that?"

She narrowed her eyes. Was this way of telling her she smelled badly? "I washed in the pitcher and basin. Is that acceptable?"

He flushed and rubbed the back of his neck. "I didn't mean that as an insult. I was thinking that a lady such as yourself would appreciate a nice leisurely bath to start out the day. I would imagine there were no facilities on the train, and...well, I just thought it might make you feel better, more at home."

Her shoulders slumped. "I'm sorry. My temper was uncalled for. That's the second time I've gotten snippy with you for no reason."

"No offense taken, Madeline. Your world has been turned upside down. A little testiness is to be expected." He winked and held out his arm. "Tell you what, let's head back to the house. Conor can handle the plowing on his own for a while. Let me give you that tour I promised."

"Are you sure? I can muddle through on my own. I hate to take you from your work."

"Positive." His eyes sparkled as he took her hand and slipped it through the crook of his arm.

Her stomach hollowed at his closeness, his scent a combination of sweat, leather, and soil. When would she no longer feel awkward around him? Off center? Thus far, he'd been gracious and understanding, exhibiting a keen intellect and sharp wit. Nothing like her parents had taught her about the Irish.

A sidelong glance caught him watching her, his expression unreadable. She ducked her head. Could he sense what she was thinking? Was he aware of her conflicting thoughts, the prejudices she struggled to set aside?

##

The breeze tugged at Seamus's collar as he led Madeline toward the barn. Sunlight glistened on her hair, setting her auburn locks on fire. He'd never seen anyone with such deep red hair. What would it look like tumbling down her back? He swallowed and forced his attention to the massive structure in front of them.

"We keep everything we use to run the farm in here, not just the animals. If we were to leave the sulky...uh...plow outside, the metal would rust in no time."

"Why is it called a sulky?"

He shrugged. "An odd name, isn't it? Someone once told me that it was invented by a sulky man who wanted to ride by himself, but the story sounds far-fetched to me."

She giggled. "That does seem rather outlandish."

"The hay and other feed are stored in here." He gestured to an open area on one side of the building, then pointed across the aisle. "And over there we keep the horses' tack, the yoke, and tools."

Her jaw hung slack as her gaze traveled up to the loft. "The barn is huge from the outside, but every space is utilized."

"We've got corrals for the horses, so they don't have to remain indoors on beautiful days like today if they're not working. And I've got some pasture land for the few cows we own. You'll meet them later when I teach you how to milk."

Madeline's gaze shot to his, and her face paled. "Milk?"

Swallowing a grin, he nodded. "You'll be fine, and I won't leave you to do it alone until you're comfortable."

"That could be a while."

"You're a smart gal and will pick up the task quicker than you think. I've got every faith in you."

"At least one of us does." She wrinkled her nose but squared her shoulders with a nod. "I'm willing to try."

"That's my brave girl." Seamus patted her hand, so soft under his calloused fingers. "Now, let's go to the cabin where the pantry, root cellar, and icehouse are."

"I don't believe I'll ever take running a household for granted. Cook procured, stored, and prepared the food. We also had a young woman who handled the laundry." She pressed her lips together. "I'm afraid I've got a lot to learn. You may regret not choosing a woman better trained."

"After seeing you with Conor, I'm willing to teach you everything else. He and the children are what's most important. We can figure out everything else."

Inside the house, he opened a trunk stuffed with piles of fabric. On top was a jar filled with buttons. A red felt ball held pins and needles. The twins have begun to outgrow their clothes, so you'll need to let out hems and waistbands as their current items will allow, but there should be plenty in here to get you started on making new garments for them.

She ran her fingers over the material, her eyes wide with...panic?

He nudged her shoulder. "You don't sew either, do you?"

"No." Her voice was barely above a whisper, and a tear rolled down her cheek. "When I was a child, I learned how to make samplers and decorative items. We had all our clothing made for us."

His heart tugged. She was overwhelmed. Wait until she discovered he'd planned to have her whitewash the inside of the house. The task was long overdue, but he never seemed to get around to it. Perhaps they could do it together. He closed the lid with a sigh. He meant what he said about his willingness to wait for her to adjust, but had the pastor who referred her realized how unprepared she was for her new life? "Let's take a break. You've had a lot to absorb. Sit at the table, and I'll bring us some coffee."

She nodded and dropped into one of the chairs near the table, then propped her chin in her hand, a look of discouragement on her face.

"Tell me about your sisters. All I know is that they are younger than you."

Her lips twisted. "They both thought I was crazy to come here. Maybe they were right."

"Nonsense." He poured their drinks, then set a mug in front of her before sitting down beside her. "You've been here a bit more than twenty-four hours. Let's give it some time." He sipped the strong dark liquid. "What do they look like? Do they have children?"

"Not yet, but Phoebe is expecting. She is tall like me, but has beautiful black hair, like a raven, and her eyes are blue. She is married to Elias. Cecelia is petite and blonde, and she also has blue eyes. Her husband is Horace." She touched her hair and frowned. "No one is sure where my red hair and brown eyes came from."

"No one else in the family has them?"

"No, so my looks were always a topic of conversation inside our own home as well as the drawing rooms of Boston."

The poor woman. Judged by others simply because of her looks. He reached out and fingered the stray lock that had pulled from her bun. As soft and silky as he'd imagined. Her eyes widened, and he dropped his hand. "Well, I think the color is stunning." He grinned. "And the good news is that you no longer need care what Boston's elite think."

Madeline snickered, and her face lost some of its shadows. Doubt and sorrow still clouded her eyes.

Heart hammering, he lifted her chin until her eyes met his. She trembled at his touch. He wanted...no, needed to make her smile, to help her shed her past hurts, and to make her feel valued for who she was, not for what she could do. "Please believe me when I say that you are a beautiful woman, not despite your hair, but because of it. More importantly, you are beautiful from the inside out. You have a gentle spirit and a steadfast faith. Just because you don't know how to be a farmwife, doesn't mean you can't learn. I will teach you what I can, but our nearest neighbor, the Brennans, will help you learn what I don't know how to teach you. And when you're ready, we'll pack our bags and return to Boston to visit your sisters."

Moisture shimmered in her eyes.

He cleared his throat. "I'm glad you're here, pleased you agreed to marry me. At some point, I'd like a...uh...real marriage, but I will not rush you." His face heated, and hers reddened. She was as embarrassed as he was, but the conversation was necessary. "The bedroom is yours alone as long as you need it. Understood?"

She nodded.

"Now, how about—"

"Seamus! Seaaaaaamuuus!" Conor's shout pierced the air.

Chapter Seven

Madeline lifted her skirts and raced out of the house behind Seamus. She squinted into the sunlight, but the glare prevented her from seeing Conor's predicament. Her breath was ragged in her ears as she ran over the uneven ground, and a sharp pang cut into her side. *Please, God, let him be uninjured.*

She slowed to a trot, and Seamus pulled ahead. Minutes later she arrived beside the sulky where he was attempting to disentangle his brother from the harness. Conor stood next to Bess, both forearms wrapped in the leather straps used to guide the horse. Mumbling as he worked, Seamus cast a glance at her and shrugged.

Tugging against the straps, Conor tried to lift his arm. He wore a deep frown, and his face was flushed. "I'm sorry, Seamus. There was a hawk chasing an oriole, and I couldn't let him win. I shouted at the birds, but they didn't pay attention to me. I guess they couldn't hear me, so I decided to see if I could find some stones to throw at the big one, to scare him off, you know. The oriole was so beautiful. But as I climbed down, my arm got caught, and then I fell, and the reins pulled tight, and I couldn't figure out how to fix it." He felt silent, and his lower lip trembled.

"You're okay, now." Madeline squeezed his shoulder. "Seamus will have you out of there in a jiffy." She watched as Seamus's long, tapered fingers worked to unknot the reins. "Can I help?"

A crease wrinkled his forehead as he nodded and pointed to one of the traces. "This piece keeps moving, so if you can hold it still, I'll see if I can't loosen the other strap so he can slide his left arm out. That should free his other arm."

She moved next to Seamus and grabbed the piece of leather he'd indicated. His breath was warm on her cheek as he worked, and his fingers occasionally brushed hers. Despite the day's heat, goose bumps raised on her arms, and her pulse fluttered. She licked her lips and tried to focus.

After several attempts, he was able to undo the snarled leather, and Conor's arms slipped from their constraints. Seamus pulled his brother into a hug and stroked his back. "That wasn't too bad, was it?"

"No." Conor's voice was muffled against Seamus's chest. "But I feel kind of silly for letting it happen. Over a stupid bird."

Seamus released his grip and chucked him lightly on the chin. "It was an accident. No need to be embarrassed. I only hope you were able to save the oriole."

"I made such a racket hollering for you, the hawk broke off pursuit."

"Well then, something good came of all this, didn't it?"

"I guess so."

"I know so." He ruffled Conor's hair.

Madeline swallowed the lump in her throat. Seamus's gentleness and patience was evidence of his love for his brother.

"How long since you had some water, Conor?"

"A while. I wanted to finish this field before taking a break."

"An admirable goal, Brother. Let me get you some while you wait here with Madeline. You can tell her about the oriole."

Conor gaped at her. "Haven't you ever seen one?"

She shook her head as Seamus hurried toward the house. "No, what do they look like?"

A smile broke out on his face, and his eyes took on a distant glaze. He spread his hand. "Their bodies are slightly larger than my palm with a wingspan of about seven inches. What I saw was a male. He had a black head and his body is an orange-yellow with black-and-white wings. People confuse them with goldfinches, but they're more of a lemon yellow."

"I can see why you wanted to save him. Do you like birds?"

"Very much." He pursed his lips and whistled. "That's what they sound like."

She clapped her hands. "Can you do other birdcalls?"

A look of triumph on his face, he grinned, then chirped. "That was a goldfinch, and I know lots of others."

"That's wonderful. You've quite a talent."

“I should have done an eagle’s cry. That would have scared off the hawk. Too bad I didn’t think of that.”

Madeline cast a glance at the heavens. *Dear Father, thank You for this special time with Conor. Thank You for keeping him safe. Is it too much to ask that You help him shed the darkness that grips him?*

##

Footsteps pounding on the ground, Seamus rushed toward his brother and Madeline, carrying a bucket and ladle. Conor was regaling her with his repertoire of birdcalls. “When he gets going, the barn sounds like an aviary.” He held the pail while Conor dipped the ladle into the water, then lifted it to his lips and drank.

“That’s good, Seamus. Thanks. I hate that you had to rescue me.”

He nudged Conor’s shoulder. “Anytime, Brother. Anytime.” He smiled at Madeline, and she blushed, the pink bringing roses to her cheeks. Her eyes sparkled, and she nibbled her lower lip. She was a beautiful and gentle woman. He’d misjudged her badly upon her arrival. How would he have acted if he’d taken an exhausting trip across the country in a crowded and cramped train with little to break up the monotony.

She stood close to his brother. “Is the water quenching your thirst? Are you feeling better?”

“Yes, I think I could finish plowing.”

Seamus shook his head. "Let's unhook Bess and let her out in the corral. You can accompany us for the rest of the tour. Then we'll grab some lunch and get back to it afterward. How's that sound?"

Relief flitted across Conor's face, and he nodded.

Madeline gazed at Seamus with gratitude and admiration, and his chest swelled. He could get used to having her look at him like that. Conor finished drinking, and she took the ladle from him, then reached for the bucket in Seamus's hand. Her fingers skimmed his, and a jolt ran up his arm. He tugged at his collar, his hand still buzzing from her touch. "Give us a hand, Conor."

Moments later, they were headed for the enclosure, Bess clip-clopping behind them. Seamus opened the gate, and the horse sauntered inside, then turned and hung her head over the fence. He rubbed her nose, and she nickered. Madeline stood back twisting her hands. He gestured for her to join him, and she took a hesitant step forward.

Conor held out his hand. "You helped me, Miss Madeline. I'll help you. There's nothing to be afraid of. Bess is sweet. She wants to say hello. That's why she's looking over the fence."

Her gaze ricocheted from Conor to the horse to him, and Seamus smiled in what he hoped was an encouraging way. She lifted her chin and gripped Conor's fingers, an expression of determination on her face as he led her toward the pen.

Seamus crossed his arms as he watched their interplay. He was proud of the efforts she was making to fit into the family. She treated his brother like an equal, never once denigrating him for his problems. Would she be as accepting and gracious with the twins? Her sisters were younger, but had she been around children? Did she know what to do with them?

Madeline rubbed the side of Bess's head, tentatively at first, then with more confidence. She giggled, and her face lit up as the horse blew out a breath and bobbed her head as if to say thank you.

His stomach rumbled. "As much fun as this is, I'm starving. How about if we head in to get something to eat? I'll put away the harness and join you in the house."

"No, we'll all go. We're on this tour together." She grinned at his brother. "Isn't that right, Conor?"

"Absolutely."

"And I suppose you'll want us all to pitch in making lunch?" He chuckled and drew his brow into an exaggerated frown. "What kind of wife are you?"

Her laughter pealed. "The kind who's going to expect you to pull your weight."

Conor slapped him on the back and guffawed. "I think you've met your match, Brother."

Seamus shrugged, warmth spreading through him. She had gumption. He'd give her that. They wandered into the barn, and he hung the harness on the wrought-iron hook near the rest of the tack.

Dahlia, one of three cows who was close to giving birth, bellowed from her stall. He rushed toward the sound and looked over the slated gate. She lay on her side, breathing heavily, her tongue lolling. How long had she been in labor? She wasn't due for another couple of weeks.

Conor startled, and Madeline's eyes were wide and frantic, her mouth in a perfect O.

He waved her away. "I'll need to stay here until she's had the calf. Take Conor inside and keep him there. He...uh..."

"I understand. Once I get him settled, I'll bring you some food. It could be a long wait." She looped arms with Conor and led him from the barn. "Now you get to show me how good a cook you are."

Their voices faded, and Seamus blew out a deep breath as he ran his fingers through his hair. As a farmwife, she should know how to birth the animals, but the last delivery had caused Conor to have another episode, and he'd been inconsolable. Fortunately, the animal had done most of the work herself, so he could focus on his brother. He wouldn't risk another incident, so it was best she remained with Conor.

Thank You, God, for a partner I can count on. Three days ago, I felt alone and ready to call it quits, but now it seems I've got someone to share the burden.

The cow lowed again, and Seamus shed his jacket and rolled up his sleeves. He'd have time to think about his new wife and their future later. Meanwhile, he had a farm to run.

Chapter Eight

Judging from the lengthening shadows, hours had passed since the heifer had begun labor. She'd done well for a first-timer, and his heart went out to the young cow. The poor thing probably didn't understand what was happening to her. He stroked her head, murmuring sounds of consolation and encouragement. About an hour ago, two more cows had gone into labor as well, but he still had time to birth this calf before attending them.

As promised, Madeline had brought him food. Not once, but twice, as well as a bucket of water and some rags, "just in case." He smiled. She was trying her best to fit in and become a true helpmeet, and he appreciated the efforts. Her eyes had filled with tears when the cow bellowed, and he'd sent her back into the house. His new wife was tenderhearted.

His back ached as he helped the bovine lie down. By all indications, she was ready. "You're doing great, girl. I'm proud of you."

The heifer's eyes rolled toward him as if she understood his words. Thirty minutes later, he welcomed a bull calf into the world, and he swallowed a lump in his throat. The wonder of birth never ceased to move him. One of God's greatest miracles. "You've got yourself a good, strong son."

She lowed and snuffled the ground, then began to tend to her new baby, licking and cleaning the calf. Bleating, he staggered to his feet, then tottered toward his mother's udder.

Seamus sighed. Another successful addition to the herd. With quick motions, he cleaned the stall, raking away the soiled straw and putting down fresh. He dumped some clover hay nearby, so the cow could begin to rebuild her strength.

Sweat dampened his shirt, and it clung to his back like a second skin. He ladled himself some water and mopped his face. One down, two to go. Would he get any sleep tonight? How was Madeline faring with Conor?

He massaged his shoulders and rotated his neck to ease some of the ache. Behind him, one of the other heifers mooed, the sound deep and insistent. He gave the cow and her calf pats on the rumps and hurried across the aisle to the enclosure. "Hang in there, girl. I'm here to help."

The moon had already started its descent by the time two more calves entered the family, and the purple fingers of dawn lightened the horizon as he finished cleaning the stalls and ensured the babies had begun to nurse. *Thank You, Father, for these new lives, for providing for us. I don't deserve Your blessings, yet You continue to shower me and mine with Your grace and mercy.*

His step was springy and eager as he made his way to the pump to wash away the dirt and grime. He stripped to the waist and scrubbed in the frigid water, shivering in the early morning coolness. He dunked his head under the spigot, then soaped his hair and rinsed off. Toweling himself dry, he donned a fresh shirt. His stomach grumbled, and he hurried toward the house. Madeline was probably sleeping, so the stove would be cold, but he could at least nibble on some bread.

He tiptoed up the steps and across the porch, then eased open the door. His gaze took in his brother curled up on the sofa asleep under a blanket, and Madeline in the rocking chair by the window. A Bible was open on her lap. Her eyes were open, and a tired smile curved her lips. "How are the new mothers and their babies?" she whispered.

"You're awake. Was there a problem with Conor?" Mindful of his brother's slumbering, Seamus trod lightly to where she sat.

"No, he nodded off a couple of hours after dinner. I couldn't help in the barn but thought some prayer might be appreciated."

"Always, and that worked. Everyone is healthy and strong." He sighed. "You waited up."

"Isn't that what a good farmwife does?" She cocked her head and grinned, then pushed herself to her feet. "And now for some breakfast."

He gaped at her. He'd underestimated his bride.

Looking pleased, Madeline grabbed his hand and led him to the table. "Sit." She pushed him into the chair, then poured a steaming mug of coffee and put it in his hands. Striking a match, she lit the stove and scrambled several eggs, then opened the oven and withdrew a plate that held fried ham and potatoes. She scraped the fluffy yellow concoction onto the plate and set it in front of him.

His mouth watered as the smoky aroma of the ham filled his nose. “It smells divine.”

Her face pink, she shrugged. “The ham is a bit charred. I’m still trying to figure out how to control the temperature in the iron skillet. First it is too hot, then too cold. The potatoes may not be cooked correctly either. I feel a bit like Goldilocks.”

He chuckled. “Does that make me one of the three bears?” He sliced the meat and forked a piece into his mouth. Dry, but flavorful. “Delicious.”

“You’re just being kind.”

“Is it perfect? No. Does it taste good? Yes.” He patted her hand. “You are making an effort, so who am I to criticize. Skills take time to learn, and you’re doing great. Remember, you’ve only been here for a few days. I’m proud of you.”

The pink in her cheeks deepened, and she nibbled her lower lip. He’d already learned she did that when uncertain.

“Besides, I stand by my comments when you first arrived. You can learn the tasks and chores, but your grace and acceptance of Conor comes naturally. Those are your most important traits. We can figure out everything else.” He scooped the eggs into his mouth. Light and fluffy, they melted on his tongue. "However, your eggs are the best I've ever tasted."

"Toward the end, that's all I could get my father to eat, so I became quite adept at preparing them. Scrambled, fried, poached, soft boiled, hard boiled, omelets. Even baked."

"Then you're way ahead of me. I tend to overcook them." He ate quickly. "Do you want to see the new calves?"

"I'd love to, but don't you want to go to bed?" Concern wrinkled her forehead. "I can wait if you need to rest."

He shook his head. "No, the day has already begun. Unless another cow goes into labor, I'll turn in early tonight to try to catch up. But there's work to be done, and sometimes a farmer goes without sleep."

"Then I'd love to visit our new babies."

Seamus grinned and wiped his mouth on the napkin. She'd said *our.* He stood and held out his hand. "To the barn."

Jumping to her feet, she nestled her hand in his palm. Small and warm, it fit perfectly.

His pulse skipped as they left the house and hastened across the yard in the growing daylight. Pink and peach streaks pushed back the plum-colored heavens. Still grasping her hand, Seamus entered the mammoth building, the earthy smell of animals, straw, and manure assaulting him. To some the odor was off-putting, but to him the scent was sweeter than any perfume.

He led her to the nearest stall where Dahlia and her calf rested.

Madeline rushed forward, her eyes wide. "Oh, how darling. Is it the boy or one of the girls?"

"That's our bull. He doesn't seem like much now on his wobbly legs, but he will be."

"He's so cute. I didn't expect that. Soft and fuzzy looking with those big brown eyes."

"Yes, even the largest animals somehow manage to look adorable when they're babies." He opened the gate and beckoned her inside. "He's as soft as he appears. You may pet him."

She hesitated, then walked toward the animals, her fingers outstretched. She touched the calf, and he mooed. She jumped back with a squeak.

Seamus chuckled. "He's saying he likes you."

"Guess I need to work on my bravery."

"You've already proven your courage." He wrapped his arm around her shoulder and moved her toward the calf. "I haven't named him or the girls yet, in case you'd like to."

Her face lit up, and she nodded. "Let me think about it."

"You could name the females after your sisters." He smirked and raised one eyebrow. "Unless you have a better idea."

"Perfect." She giggled, her laughter reminding him of wind chimes he'd heard once.

"Phoebe and Cecelia it is. Let's go let them know."

After a last pat on the calf's head, she tilted her head. "I've got it. How about Ulysses after our president?"

"Our little man does look rather sure of himself. Ulysses it is." He beamed at her. "You're brilliant."

She blushed again and shuffled her foot in the straw.

He looked forward to making her blush with happiness as the days passed.

Chapter Nine

Madeline dried the last pane, then peered at the glass from various angles to determine if she'd left any streaks. An overcast day would have been a better choice to clean the windows instead of a morning filled with sunshine that evaporated the sharp-smelling vinegar as fast as she applied it. But she'd finished the rest of the housework, and Seamus hadn't arrived home with the twins, so she'd attacked the chore in an effort to pass the time while she waited.

She rehung the curtains, and they fluttered in the breeze that wafted through the opening. She blew out a deep sigh and peeked outside. No sign of the wagon. Her stomach clenched, and she pressed a hand against her middle. Had they run into problems on the journey? Was Seamus having to convince the children to come home? How did they feel about yet another mail-order bride entering their lives?

Too bad Conor was out in the fields. His company would have helped quell her nerves. But springtime was planting time, and he didn't have time to babysit her. Besides, she'd have to get used to being alone with the twins sooner rather than later.

Her gaze went to the stack of schoolbooks she'd found in a small crate next to the only upholstered chair in the house. Dusty with misuse, the McGuffey Readers had brought back memories of her own childhood. First published in 1836 and named for the man who'd created them, the books taught most of the nation how to read. She'd wiped down each one, tracing the words on the cover with gentle fingers.

With no textbooks for math, she was on her own, and numbers were not her forte. She hadn't spoken to Seamus, but perhaps he could help. After all, he'd have had to use calculations to build the addition to his parents' house and the barn. She could get the twins started with basic addition and subtraction, but once they got past the times tables, she would flounder. Arithmetic and other school subjects hadn't been part of her lessons.

Instead, she'd been groomed for society. The proper way to dress, eat, and talk. How to manage a house full of servants. She snorted a laugh as she looked around. No staff here.

Did Seamus really believe she was the right woman? She'd cleaned house and fumbled through the laundry, but her cooking was not good, with food undercooked, scorched, or a combination of both. Her face scorched. He'd been polite and encouraging, but he must be disappointed in her abilities. Her caring for Conor would only go so far. Eventually, Seamus would expect her to be as skilled as the other farmwives. Would she be able to learn all she needed?

Wagon wheels rattled outside, and she rushed to the door, her heart hammering in her chest. They were home. She shielded her eyes against the sun's glare and studied the small girl and boy seated next to Seamus.

Both children had jet-black hair and fair complexions. pixie-like with heart-shaped faces and close features, they were slender. Bouncing on the wooden bench of the buckboard, they chattered like magpies. Seamus nodded and leaned close as if they were telling him the most important thing he'd ever heard.

Her mouth dried, and she swallowed. Straightening her spine, she lifted a hand in greeting. Were children like animals? Did they sense fear? If so, she'd have to work to squelch her doubts. She forced a smile.

The wagon came to a halt, and he waved. "Ho, there!" He jumped down and lifted each of the children to the ground. He wrapped his arms around their shoulders. "Madeline, I'd like you to meet Kathleen and Kagan."

She gripped the railing and descended the stairs, praying she wouldn't trip or fall flat on her face. Addressing a roomful of socialites was less terrifying. "How do you do?"

"You talk funny." Kathleen's lips twisted. "And your hair is a weird color."

"Kathleen." Seamus's voice held an edge of warning. "Be nice."

"What?" Kathleen's eyes were wide. "You and Daddy said I must always tell the truth."

Madeline's heart dropped. Not quite six years old, and the child would have bested some of the most haughty of socialites. "I'm from Boston, and our accent is quite strong. As for my hair, it's the color God gave me, so you'll have to speak to Him about it."

The girl had the grace to blush but didn't apologize.

"Kagan, don't you have anything to say?" Seamus stroked the boy's head.

"Uh, hi." He stuffed his hands in the pockets of his short pants. "Where's Daddy?"

"He's working the back field." Madeline gestured toward the horizon. "He and your uncle have been plowing while you've been gone."

"Of course they are. It's springtime. Don't you know anything?" Kathleen smirked.

"Kath—"

"Not about Iowa, and certainly not about farming." Madeline cut off Seamus's reproof. "I guess you'll have to teach me. Would you be willing to do that?"

Kathleen stared at her long and hard, emotions warring for supremacy on her face. She finally shrugged. "Maybe, but you're not my mother, and you can't tell me what to do."

"No, I'm not your mother, but I do expect you to follow my directions. Just like you do for your uncle even though he's not your father."

"All right." Kathleen's displeasure was evident from her frown, but she'd apparently decided she wasn't going to win today's argument.

One battle over. Many more to come. Madeline held out her hands. "Now, if you'll come inside. I baked some cookies, and you must be hungry after your long ride."

Kagan tucked his hand in hers, but Kathleen marched past ignoring her proffered fingers.

Seamus pulled their satchels from the back of the wagon and set them on the ground. "I'll put up the horse and wagon and be in after a while. You enjoy your cookies and getting to know each other." He met Madeline's gaze over the boy's head and winked. Warmth filled her. It would be a long road with the little girl, but his action told her he would walk beside her.

##

The sun was at its zenith above, but a light breeze ruffling Seamus's hair took the sting out of the heat. Putting away the wagon and taking care of the mare had taken longer than anticipated. As he'd led her into the barn, she'd picked up a stone in her hoof, and he spent the better part of fifteen minutes trying to dislodge the irritant.

How was Madeline handling kids? Shy Kagan seemed to like her well enough, or perhaps his emotions were in anticipation of the sweet treats. No, the boy was an even-keeled child who accepted anyone who crossed his path. On the other hand, Kathleen seemed to take pride in being difficult. Were her behaviors the result of her mother's death or her father's issues or his own inabilities to raise a little girl? Or was her nastiness inbred? Would she ever become a sweet, pliant girl?

He hurried across the yard and trotted up the stairs onto the porch. Through the window he could hear Madeline shriek. He shoved open the door and froze.

She stood near the stove, her wide eyes staring at a large squashed spider on the floor. She raised her face, and with an imperceptible shake of her head, she met his gaze. "Everything all right in the barn?"

"Yes, the mare picked up a stone, but I was able to remove it." He narrowed his eyes and studied the children. Kagan sat on the couch swinging his legs and smiling at Seamus. His twin stood near the sofa, arms crossed and a look of triumph on her face. When she saw him, her smirk lost its edge, and her gaze slid toward the floor. Did she have something to do with the spider's appearance, or was she simply enjoying Madeline's fearful reaction?

Tromping to the sink, he washed his hands as he sniffed the air. "Smells wonderful in here. Is that chicken baking?"

As anticipated, the pink flush stained Madeline's cheeks. Why did she embarrass so easily when he complimented her? Had she never received praise for a job well done?

"Yes, and I'm roasting potatoes, carrots, and parsnips. I poked them with a fork, and they seem soft enough, so I think they're cooked correctly this time." She gave him a resigned grin as she shrugged.

He dried his hands, then squeezed her arm. "I'm sure lunch will be delicious, and you've obviously worked hard on it." He wheeled and pierced the kids with his gaze. "And what do we say when we're grateful?"

"Thank you." Kagan's voice rang out, but Kathleen's mumbled response was barely audible.

Madeline caught his eye, and he pressed his lips together. She was obviously determined to handle the situation with Kathleen on her own. She was probably right. If he continued to step in, Kathleen would never respect her.

"You're welcome. Now, come sit down and eat while the food is hot." She bustled between the oven and the table, setting out the dishes, then pouring water into their glasses. A light sheen of perspiration dampened her face, making her glow in the sunlight pouring through the window. "Is Conor coming?"

"No, he's going to work for a while longer." Seamus hung up the towel and waited until she'd finished serving before helping her into her chair. She smiled her thanks, and his chest swelled. Only four days with them, and he couldn't imagine their lives without her. How did she feel, especially now that the twins were back? He lowered himself in the chair, then grasped Kathleen's and Madeline's hands. Both were small and warm in his palm. "Dear Father God, thank You for the food You provide for us. Bless Madeline for preparing it. Thank You for sending her to us. Be with us as we get to know each other and become a family. Amen."

He forked a parsnip chunk into his mouth and moaned. His eyes widened. Savory flavors coated his mouth. "You've outdone yourself."

"Thank you. I...uh...found some jars of dried herbs in the root cellar. I'm glad you like it."

Kagan poked vegetable chunks into his mouth until his cheeks bulged like a squirrel preparing for winter. Apparently, he was enjoying the meal as well. Kathleen fiddled with her food, pushing it around on her plate. Should he say something to the child, or would that exacerbate her orneriness?

Madeline turned to Kagan. "Did you have fun staying with your friends?"

He lit up and in between bites talked about climbing trees, playing hide-n-seek, and tossing sticks to the family's dog. "Ivy's is going to have puppies soon, Uncle Seamus. Can we have one of them? A dog would be good to have, don't you think? He could help us on the farm."

"You've given this some thought, haven't you?" Seamus smiled. "And I agree with you. Mark Brennan told me about the anticipated litter at church a couple of weeks ago, and I think a dog would make a wonderful addition to the family."

The boy clapped his hands. "Thanks, Uncle Seamus. We're getting a puppy, Kathleen."

"Yeah, whatever. You can have him. I'm not interested in a smelly, dirty dog. Make sure you keep him out of our room."

"But I want him to sleep with me."

"Forget it."

Kagan's lower lip trembled.

Seamus wiped his mouth. "I'm sure we can work out something to please everyone. Now, I know you're too old for naps, but I'd like you to lie down in your rooms for a bit. I have a feeling you didn't sleep much while you were gone, and the ride home was long."

Kathleen looked mulish but didn't argue. Instead, she rose, kissed him on the cheek, and trudged toward the bedroom. Kagan clambered from the chair and followed his sister.

"I'll go tuck them in." Madeline rose, a determined look on her face.

Was she going to take the opportunity to reprimand the children?

She slipped into their room, and he strained to listen. Sheets rustled, and he imagined her pulling the covers over the kids.

"Why didn't you yell at us or tattle to Uncle Seamus about what we did?" Kathleen's tone held suspicion.

"Because raised voices rarely solve a problem, and what happened is between the two of you and me. There's no reason to get him involved. I know we're going to be friends, and friends work things out between themselves. How does that sound?"

"Good." A sniffle, then Kathleen said, "I'm sorry for being mean."

"Yeah, we're sorry," Kagan piped up.

"You're forgiven. And we won't give it another thought. Sleep tight."

Seamus crossed his arms and grinned. Perhaps Kathleen had finally met her match.

Chapter Ten

Madeline descended the porch steps and sauntered toward the barn. A week had passed since the twins returned home, and she'd settled into an uneasy truce with Kathleen. The little girl was alternately sweet and sassy, walking a fine line between civility and bad behavior. She knew better than to pull any stunts when Seamus was around, but there were plenty of times he was out of the house.

When an invitation had come for the children to spend the weekend with their friends, Madeline was relieved Seamus agreed to the arrangement. She had made headway with the child, but a long road lay ahead. Fortunately, she was years away from the terrible teens.

A breeze thick with the odor of hay, manure, and freshly turned soil stroked her cheeks and ran its fingers through her hair. So different from the coal-scented air in Boston. The noises contrasted too. Rain on the tin roof. Hooves plodding, trotting, or galloping. The wood frame on the windmill creaking. And the animals...horses whinnying, cows mooing, chickens clucking, and the stuttering laugh of the goats. She'd been headbutted by one of the creatures yesterday when she went out to collect eggs. A painful lesson to learn, but now she knew not to turn her back on the critters.

She finished the household chores, and the idea of wrestling with the treadle on the sewing machine to make the kids' clothes held no allure, so she'd given herself the morning off. Seamus and Conor had packed sandwiches for lunch so they could work until they finished preparing the last field for planting. The land was beautiful, but how did they stand the everyday tedium of turning over acres of dirt?

He promised her they'd start on her vegetable garden tomorrow, so she'd have her own plot to care for. What if she couldn't make anything grow? Would she be the only farmwife in history to fail to feed her family? Cook had had a tiny garden in the backyard. Too bad Madeline hadn't thought to ask for advice, but growing produce was the last thing on her mind when she'd fled.

Sunlight was warm on her shoulders as she searched the brown expanse for Seamus and Conor...her husband and brother-in-law...two terms she never thought she'd use with affection. How quickly life had changed.

What were Phoebe and Cecelia doing? Did they miss her, or were they caught up in the daily activities of their own families?

Movement in the east field caught her attention, and she watched the men guide the plow through the dirt. The weather had held thus far, and Seamus was pleased with the progress they'd made. Something else that didn't enter her mind in Massachusetts: the elements. Rain had been an irritant, not a wished-for event to soak newly planted ground or a worry if precipitation failed to materialize. Here, too little rain was an issue as was too much, although he'd said it had been years since a major flood had occurred.

She sauntered toward the pasture where the cows grazed. With a soft moo, the calf she'd named Phoebe trotted toward the fence. Madeline smiled to see the awkward animal who seemed to be all legs make her way through the herd. She poked her head through the slots, sniffing at Madeline's hand. She petted the heifer's head, and her chest swelled. Her comfort with the animals was increasing by the day. "You're getting so big." The calf bleated as if she understood.

A bellow came from across the pasture, and the calf cast a glance over its shoulder, then turned and loped toward the bawl. The mother had called its baby who recognized the sound. Madeline's eyes widened. To her the noises were indistinguishable. Was Seamus able to differentiate? She blew out a sigh. So much to learn.

Moving away from the cows, she headed toward the next pasture. Vacant, the large pen was filled with swaying grass and wildflowers. Purple, yellow, and pink blooms bobbed in the wind. She snapped her fingers and hurried back to the house to retrieve a basket. The flowers would spruce up the living quarters, and she and the kids could learn about them together.

Bearing two flat willow baskets she'd found in the root cellar, she smiled and slipped through the fence slats. Bees danced among the stalks of colorful blossoms, and she waved them away. Time passed as she ambled toward a copse of trees in the center of the field, collecting a variety of flowers.

Perspiration stuck her hair to the sides of her face, and dampened her bodice. She'd seen Cook create small bundles of herbs and flowers and hang them upside down in the pantry. Was drying flowers as easy as it appeared? Surely she could manage this small task without bothering the men.

The image of Seamus's face pushed its way into her mind. His green eyes the color of newly mown grass and crinkling at the corners when he smiled her. The lock of dark blond hair that habitually fell over his forehead. Her pulse quickened. Did he realize how handsome he was? He didn't have the arrogance of most of the good-looking men who frequented Boston's drawing rooms, wearing silk jackets and strutting like peacocks.

Instead, he walked with fluid grace, his limbs loose and his broad shoulders straining against his shirt when he moved. His angular face and hands tanned from hours in the sun. His fingers were long and tapered, strong when he was working the farm, gentle when he stroked the children's hair. Her breath caught. What would his hands feel like on her hair?

Hooves thundered, and she glanced toward the rumble. A massive black horse galloped toward her, its eyes wide and rolling. Mouth open, it brayed and snorted as it charged.

Madeline froze, her heart pounding in her chest. Her feet refused to move as if nailed to the ground, yet her knees trembled and threatened to give way. She clutched the basket as if a lifeline. Where did the horse come from?

The animal ate up the distance, squealing as it approached. A few short yards away, it stopped and reared, towering above her.

Nausea roiled in her gut, and her breath came in gasps. Black pinpricks danced in her vision. Would the animal attack her? Could she make it to the trees, or would running agitate the beast even more?

A shrill whistle shrieked, then the crack of a gunshot. The horse came down on all fours and shook its head. Rearing again, it danced in place.

Footsteps pounded, and Madeline slid her gaze toward the sound. Seamus raced toward them, gun in one hand and a lasso in the other. He swung the rope. Around and around and around. Then he tossed the lasso, and the coil sailed through the air and encircled the horse's neck. The mighty animal balked against the constraint, but Seamus clung to the cord and sank to the ground. Sides heaving, the horse's head dropped.

Madeline crumpled. Darkness enveloped her.

Chapter Eleven

Deep voices murmured and seemed to come from far away, but Madeline couldn't grasp the words. Where was she? Hard ground pressed against her back, and the sun's glare filtered through her eyelids. She blinked, then closed her eyes against the piercing light. Something stroked her cheek, and she tilted her face toward the touch.

The vision of a rearing horse flooded into her mind, and she gasped.

"You're safe now." Gentle hands grasped her hands.

She cracked her eyelids. Seamus's face came into view, then Conor's behind him. Both wearing expressions of concern. Images materialized: the horse charging, then rearing, Seamus capturing the animal, then...nothing. When she realized she was no longer in danger, she'd fainted. Heat suffused her face. What kind of farmwife fainted at the first sign of trouble? The men must be disgusted at her timidity.

Struggling to sit up, her stomach lurched, and she swallowed. Losing her breakfast would only add to her humiliation. She lay back down with a groan.

"Conor, please get her some water."

Footsteps faded.

Seamus brushed hair away from her forehead, then slid his arm under her shoulders. “Okay, we’re going to do this nice and slow.”

Teeth caught between her lips, she nodded.

He eased her into an upright position, stopping periodically to let her get her equilibrium. His arm remained around her, giving her support. “Nothing appears to be broken, but you may have some bruises from the fall.”

Eyes downcast, she nodded again. Why couldn’t she make her mouth work? Words tumbled through her head, but she couldn’t seem to form sentences.

With his index finger, he lifted her chin until her gaze met his. “I sense that you’re embarrassed over what happened, but you shouldn’t be. A stallion of that size is impressive, but to face him head-on when he’s angry is terrifying. You have nothing to be ashamed of.”

“But it wouldn’t have happened if I wasn’t in the wrong place. Is the horse okay? I didn’t mean to get him in trouble.”

Seamus chuckled and tucked a lock of hair behind her ear. “Midnight is fine, and he’s not in trouble. I had Conor take him to the barn. This whole thing is my fault. He’s a new horse, and still a little territorial. I failed to tell you where on the property it was safe to go.”

Conor hurried toward them carrying a glass of water. “Are you all right, Madeline? Did you hurt yourself?”

She smiled and took the glass from him. "I'm fine, Conor. Just a bit banged up but nothing that won't heal. I'm sorry to take you men from your work. You have enough to do without worrying about me. I guess I should just stick close to the house."

"No, that wouldn't be fair. We'll be sure to tell you which fields are off limits each morning." Conor cuffed Seamus's head. "Won't we, Brother?"

"Yes, lesson learned." He turned to Madeline. "Do you feel well enough to stand, so we can get you onto the porch?"

"I think so." She spied her baskets. "I need my flowers. That's why I was in the field. I thought I'd liven up the house with some blooms and was going to try my hand at drying some of them."

"And so you shall after you've had a chance to rest."

She finished the water and returned the glass to Conor, enjoying the feel of Seamus's arm around her. His scent of leather, dirt, and perspiration sent her pulse skittering, and her face warmed again. He helped her climb to her feet, and she swayed. His gripped tightened. Her vision cleared, and she held up her hands. "I'm fine. Thank you."

"That may be, but you're trembling, so I'll support you until you're seated."

"All right." Little did he know that it was his closeness and not the incident that had caused her body to quiver.

Conor picked up the baskets, and Seamus guided her through the field, then helped her climb through the slats. They walked to the house, her steps more sure as they progressed. He lowered her onto the rocker, and Conor took her flowers inside.

"I'm sorry for all the upheaval I've caused."

"Nonsense. This wouldn't have happened if I had informed you about Midnight. No more apologies. You rest for a bit, and I'll keep you company."

"I don't understand how you were there. When I first entered the pasture, you and Conor were in the east field, plowing."

He finger-combed his hair. "This is going to sound crazy, but I got the sense that something was amiss. At first, the feeling was just niggling, like a fly pestering me, but then the perception got stronger, so I headed toward the house. That's when I saw Midnight."

"But where did you get the rope? Surely, you don't carry a lasso while plowing."

"No, I'd left it on the fence when I put him out this morning."

Conor came out of the house and squeezed her shoulder. "I'm gonna head back to the field. Sure am glad you're okay, Madeline." His boots clomped down the steps, and he strolled away.

"You should go help him."

Seamus shook his head. "He'll be fine. I'd like to keep you company for a bit. You still seem a bit...brittle."

Madeline shrugged. He was being so kind despite the fact she continued to prove her unsuitability toward farm life in Iowa. Every task she attempted ended in mediocrity at best and failure at worst. Should she ask if he wanted an annulment? The man deserved a better wife.

##

Seamus sat in the rocker next to Madeline's chair, then reached for her hand and laced their fingers. Her palm nestled against his, sending tingles into his wrist. She didn't pull away, and he stretched out his legs. The scar tissue on his back throbbed from wrestling with the horse and throwing his himself to the ground in an effort to gain leverage with the animal. He shifted on the seat and winced.

She frowned. "Did you hurt yourself saving me?"

"Nothing serious."

"But you did sustain an injury?"

"No. I...uh...have some scar tissue from during the war, and if I move the wrong way or strain that area of my back, pain is the result. I'll be fine in a day or two."

Her face paled. "I didn't realize you'd been wounded."

"Chancellorsville, but I'd rather not talk about it."

"Of course. I'm sorry."

He twisted his lips. "It's me who should be sorry. I didn't mean to bite off your head. At some point, we should discuss it, but not today." He smiled. "Today is about making you feel better."

"Sitting here is a good start. You did well placing the house. The view is spectacular."

His inhaled a deep breath. His land was beautiful, and he was pleased she felt its allure. Coming from a bustling city with all its amenities, she was sure to feel bereft. Instead, she seemed to embrace the remote plains. "I'm glad you like it, but I can't take credit for the house. My parents built it before Conor and I were born. We repaired it after the fire, but my father placed the structure."

"I hear the love in your voice for your folks. I'm sorry I didn't get to meet them."

"They were special people. I wish I could have been here to save them."

"I didn't mean to make you sad."

"You didn't. I miss them terribly, but there are many happy memories to sustain me. They were God-fearing people, so I know they're with their Savior now. Reveling in the joys of heaven rather than toiling here on earth."

"You get your faith from them."

He nodded. "We didn't always make it to church, but my father read from the Bible after dinner every night, and we held worship services on the Sundays we had to remain home. I had a happy childhood."

Madeline sighed and tried to extricate her fingers.

He sent her a sidelong glance but held on to her hand. "Yours was less so, but I hope to provide happiness for you now."

"Why? I can't possibly be the right woman for you."

His head whipped toward her. "We're both believers. We need to trust that God has worked out this arrangement. Do you have all the skills of an Iowa farmgirl? No, but I didn't have all the skills either. I'd helped my father while growing up, but then I went off to war, and after I came home I had to figure things out. On my own. Trust me when I say I made lots of mistakes."

Seamus cleared his throat and rubbed the back of her hand with his thumb. "You're smart. You can learn what you need to know. But what can't be taught is the gentle firmness you show with the children and with Conor. That is a gift, and I appreciate your abilities from the bottom of my heart."

Her cheeks were stained with pink, and tears clung to her lashes. "Thank you for saying that. I'll try not to get discouraged. It's just that...well, I don't want you to regret agreeing to marry me."

"That will never happen."

A wry smile twisted her lips. "You say that now."

He chuckled and handed her his handkerchief. "Hey, you haven't burned anything today, and everyone is safe."

She laughed, and they fell into a companionable silence.

Tension slid from his shoulders, and he closed his eyes. *Dear God, thank You for sending Madeline to us. Please help me convince her I want her here. Help me grow to love her as I should.* The words had barely evaporated in his mind when a thought sprang forward. She said she loved to read, and his paltry collection probably contained little of interest to her.

Surely there was someone in the town who could help him obtain books for her. His heart lightened. Yes, he'd start with books. A small gesture, but hopefully one that would bring her joy.

Chapter Twelve

Pastor Nairn murmured the benediction, and Madeline sighed. The service had been a balm for her weary soul. Five days had passed since the incident with Midnight, and Seamus made it a point to inform her about the locations on the property to avoid for the day. The twins had returned from spending the night with their friends. Rambunctious and keyed up, they'd had trouble settling down to schoolwork. Complaints and moaning followed every instruction she gave them. She'd held her ground, but her resolve was slipping.

When she'd opened her eyes this morning and realized it was Sunday, she'd nearly wept in relief. Chores would be kept to a minimum, and meals would be simple. She'd been ready to leave for the tiny church building an hour ahead of time. Her lips curved. No, she wasn't anxious to get out of the house.

Seamus rose, and the twins vaulted from their seats. He turned and met her eyes above their heads. "I've got to see someone. Do you mind watching Kagan and Kathleen until I'm ready to leave?"

She swallowed a frown and nodded. "We'll be outside, so they can stretch their legs before the trip home."

"Thank you. I don't expect to be too long." He bent and gathered the twins to him. Conor hadn't joined the family, preferring to remain at the farm. "Obey Madeline, and I'll meet you at the wagon."

Kathleen crossed her arms and wrinkled her nose. "I'm hungry. Can't you do whatever it is another time?"

Madeline pressed her lips together. Would Seamus address the girl's sass? Her words weren't terribly disrespectful, but her stance spoke volumes.

"We're all hungry, Katie-girl, and I must handle this immediately."

"Fine." The child whirled, grabbed her brother's hand, and dragged him outside.

Close to Kathleen's heels, Madeline held up her skirt and followed the pair into the sunshine. She squinted against the glare. "Kathleen, don't stray too far, so your Uncle Seamus won't have to find you when we're ready to leave."

The youngster pivoted, a scowl on her face. "You can't tell us what to do. You're not our mother."

Her words sliced Madeline's heart, but she straightened her spine. "No, but I am an adult and have responsibility for you. Seamus might tolerate your behavior, but I will not. You don't have to like me, but you do have to treat me with respect as you would any other grown-up. Is that understood?"

Kathleen glared at her for a long moment, then uncertainty flitted through her eyes before a mask settled into place. "Yes." She flounced toward a group of children squatting in the dirt playing jacks. She said something, and the kids turned to stared at Madeline.

She gritted her teeth. *Dear God, please help me get through to that little girl. Don't let my anger at her actions cloud my love.* A sense of warmth blanketed her, and she exhaled. *Thank You, Father.* The poor little girl had lost her mother, and her father's erratic behavior created tension and confusion. Madeline was the fourth woman to show up in less than a year, bringing more change. No wonder the child lashed out.

Chattering and laughter surrounded Madeline as families wandered across the lawn to their wagons and horses. Several people waved or stopped to introduce themselves. The tightness in her shoulders drained away. They were warm and friendly, albeit curious to see the latest mail-order bride. Did they know she and Seamus had already married? Or were they waiting for her to hightail it out of Cedar Rapids?

The church doors opened, and Seamus walked outside with a slender, dark-haired woman. She wore a cobalt-blue dress and matching hat. She laid her arm on his and laughed. Heads close together, they continued to talk for a bit, Seamus nodding periodically.

Madeline's heart skittered. Who was the woman? The two certainly seemed well acquainted. Her stomach clenched, and perspiration broke out on her face. Why hadn't he married the woman in blue? Were they more than friends? She turned away and closed her eyes. What had she gotten herself into?

##

"You're the best, Ida. I appreciate your help." Seamus shoved his hat onto his head and smiled at the petite woman on the church steps. Widowed after her husband was killed in a cattle stampede, she'd remained in Cedar Rapids. A voracious reader, she'd convinced the townspeople of the importance of a lending library. She'd raised a significant amount of money to purchase books and was in the process of setting up the library in the back of the general store. As soon as he'd decided on his surprise for Madeline, he knew Ida would be the perfect coconspirator.

"Anytime, Seamus." She squeezed his arm. "I hope things work out for you. It's been a difficult few years for the family. I'll be praying for you."

"Thank you." He tucked his hands into his pockets and rocked on his heels. "I'm optimistic. She's hardier than she appears. Katie is giving her a run for her money, but Madeline is holding her own. Kagan is so easygoing that he's already accepted her."

"Give Kathleen time. Even as young as she is, she may not like another hen in the henhouse. What about Conor?"

"Madeline has been remarkable. She doesn't fear him, and she's handled the couple of...uh...incidents with grace and aplomb. We've been working sunup to sundown, so he's bushed. He stayed home today, but plans to attend church next Sunday."

"That's wonderful. You deserve some happiness. There has been too much sorrow in your life."

"How about you? It's been three years. You're also entitled to some joy."

She shook her head. "I'm quite content on my own. I don't see myself ever falling in love again."

"You're a lovely woman, Ida. Pretty, sweet, and caring. Any man would be lucky to call you his wife."

"Smooth talker." She threw back her head and laughed. "Now, get along with you. Your bride is waiting, and she looks none too pleased. I'll be in touch when the books arrive."

"Okay." He trotted down the steps and across the grass toward the buckboard. Kathleen and Kagan sat in the back, whispering between themselves, and Madeline sat on the bench, ramrod straight. Had something occurred between her and Katie? He forced a smile. "Let's take to the road."

He climbed into the wagon and dropped onto the seat. With a slap of the reins on the horse's rump, he clicked his tongue. The conveyance lurched forward and rolled down Main Street. Madeline bumped into his arm, the warmth of her body soaking through his sleeve. Tingles traveled to his hands, and he gripped the traces. "Did you enjoy the church service? Pastor Nairn always preaches a good sermon."

"Yes."

Eyebrow raised, he shot her a glance. "Everything okay?"

"Fine. Why?"

"You seem a bit tense, that's all."

She shrugged.

What in the world had her riled up? Seamus jerked his head toward the twins. "Something happen with the kids?"

"No worse than usual. I had to correct Kathleen, and she didn't like it, but we're still making our way."

"I could talk to her."

"No. If I don't handle her, she'll never respect me. These things take time."

"Okay, but let me know if you decide you want me to intervene."

He fell silent as the buckboard continued to bump and sway. His mind raced. Husbands and wives were supposed to discuss problems. Granted, he and Madeline were married in name only at this point, but didn't she trust him enough to share her concerns? They'd had a couple of in-depth conversations at night after everyone retired, but they still barely knew each other.

The homestead came into view, and he blew out a sigh. "Look, I can tell something is upsetting you. It might be good to talk about it. Was someone rude? Or is it because I kept you all waiting? We need to be able to talk out our problems."

"No one was impolite. We don't have an issue."

Seamus slapped the reins, and the horse picked up speed. The sooner he got them home the better. He might not know women, but her mouth was drawn into a slash, and that meant something had her agitated. "If this marriage is going to work, we have to be honest with each other."

"Agreed, and you need to heed your own advice." She crossed her arms. "Stop the wagon. I'd like to walk the rest of the way."

"What?"

"I need to clear my head. We can see the house from here. Please stop. I want to get out."

"But—"

"Stop the wagon." She started to rise.

He grabbed her arm with one hand and pulled on the reins with the other. "Whoa. You can't get out while we're moving." The buckboard halted.

With some difficulty, she climbed down and began to stride toward the cabin, her face flushed and her eyes glittering with anger.

Why wouldn't she tell him what was wrong? He watched as she marched across the uneven dirt lane.

"Uncle Seamus, is Miss Madeline mad at us? We did everything she told us." Kagan stood and clambered into the seat beside him. "Is she going to leave like the other ladies did?"

Seamus scrubbed at his face. "I'm fairly certain I'm the reason she's upset. Don't worry. She's here to stay." Wasn't she?

Chapter Thirteen

Halfway between the buckboard and the house, Madeline's steps faltered. The wind cooled her hot face and tugged at her hair. Her skirt rustled as she marched across the undulating landscape. It was bad enough she'd lost her temper with Seamus, but to let the children see her anger was unconscionable.

She shoved her hands into the pockets of her dress. A lump formed in her throat, and she swallowed. *Father, I've made a mess of things, and I don't know how to fix it. Please help me make amends to this small, hurting family. Forgive my anger with Seamus for speaking to the woman at church. He didn't marry me for love but to help him. I have no right to his feelings.*

Shrieking, a hawk swooped overhead in the cloudless, cornflower-blue sky. The sun pierced the ground with unseasonably relentless heat. She plucked her perspiration-dampened bodice away from her skin and straightened her spine. Seamus provided her with a place to live and food on the table. In exchange, she would take care of the house, the kids, and his brother. God would be the love of her life. Perhaps over time Seamus would grow to feel some affection toward her.

The image of the woman in blue swam before her, and Madeline looked down at her serviceable cotton dress. She caught her teeth between her lips. As long as the comely lady in the expensive clothing was within reach, Seamus wouldn't possibly feel tenderness toward Madeline. She'd have to settle for contentment.

Chest tight, she stepped onto the porch. No one was in sight. He'd had time to put away the buckboard. She patted her hair and smoothed her skirt, then forced a smile. She opened the door and walked inside.

Seated on the couch, Seamus and the kids turned toward her, expectation and wariness on their faces. He jumped up. "We waited lunch for you."

"Thank you. That was very kind...and unexpected. I'll just wash my hands, and we can eat. Conor?"

"Take your time. Conor has already eaten." He gestured for the twins to take their place at the table where dishes, utensils, and napkins had been set. On the way to the stove he squeezed her shoulder.

A shiver snaked down her arm, and she trembled. She soaped her hands, delaying the moment when she'd have to sit down and apologize to the trio. Heat suffused her face, and she shook her head. Hopefully, they would forgive her.

Behind her, Seamus pulled pans from the oven and set them on the table. Then silence.

She'd stalled as long as she could. She rinsed her hands, then dried them and hung the towel on the hook by the window. She pivoted on her heel and froze. He stood behind her chair, a look of invitation on his face. She hurried to him and lowered herself on the seat. Even through it all, he was a gentleman. “Thank you,” she murmured as he scooted the chair close to the table. She glanced at the kids who watched the proceedings, slack jawed. Since when was Kathleen mute?

Seamus poured water into their glasses, then sat down. He extended his arms, and she grasped his hand as he asked the blessing. Afterwards, he smiled. “I hope leftovers are okay.”

Mouth dry, she nodded, then licked her lips. “First, I’d like to apologize for my anger. Losing my temper was uncalled for, and I’m sorry.”

“Are you going to leave us, Miss Madeline?” Kagan’s forehead was creased. “We didn’t mean to make you mad.”

Hands clenched together in her lap, Madeline shook her head. “I’m not going anywhere, Kagan. You aren’t to blame for my behavior.”

“Uncle Seamus says it’s his fault.” Kathleen cocked her head. “What did he do?”

“Eat your lunch, Katie-girl. Madeline and I will discuss this later, and you and your brother will be informed if necessary.”

Madeline’s stomach buzzed as if a flock of hummingbirds had taken flight. She pressed her hand against her middle. Would she be able to choke down her meal? She cleared her throat. “What would you kids like to do this afternoon? Is it too hot for you to play outside?”

Kagan bounced in his chair. "Can we go to swimming, Uncle Seamus?"

"We'll see. Just because we've had a couple of warm days doesn't mean the water isn't still cold. After all, it's only April. How about if we take our fishing poles?"

"Yuck." Kathleen's mouth twisted. "I'm going to play with my doll."

Seamus wiped his mouth with his napkin and grinned. "That sounds like fun, too. Your dad is going to stay here and take care of the animals, then come join us. It will be our turn tonight to feed and milk them."

"The work is never done, is it?" Madeline pushed a piece of beef around on her plate. "You never get a break from responsibility."

He shrugged. "A farmer's life isn't easy, but it is satisfying, and we take our fun when we can." He leveled his gaze on her. "As I said before, I'll try to make arrangements for you to visit your sisters when the time is right."

"Thank you, but there's no hurry. I need to get settled here." Her back stiffened. She had no place with Phoebe and Cecelia. Her sisters had husbands and fine places to live. They'd maintained their place in society, and she'd be a fifth wheel. Even more out of place as a newly minted farmwife. No, she didn't need to go back to Boston.

What if Father hadn't gotten ill and died? Would she have remained single and held the role of his hostess? Like when President

Tyler's daughter-in-law Priscilla and President Jefferson's daughter had acted as first ladies. Or would he have made a suitable match for her to some well-do-to member of their set?

Uzziah's smug face came to mind, and she shuddered. Fortunately, he hadn't paired her with his business partner. Her heart clenched at the thought of him living in her home. Holding court as if he'd earned the house through his own hard work rather than her father's. The man's hands touching their furniture or sitting at their table, using their dishes.

Why hadn't Father remembered to change his will leaving the property to her? She was an intelligent and capable woman. Too many men thought women didn't understand business or finance, but Father had taught her the basics. Even with her difficulties in math, she'd managed the household accounts with success, balancing quality and cost. She could have easily handled home ownership.

"Madeline?"

"I'm sorry, what?"

"Are you all right? If you're finished eating, the kids and I are ready to head outside."

"Yes...I'm sorry...I was woolgathering. You three get what you need, and I'll make quick work of the dishes. Must do my part, you know."

"You can leave them until later, if you'd like."

"No, I'd rather not come home to chores." She stood and picked up the soiled dishes, carrying them to the sink.

He rose and started to help, but she waved him away. “Go. I won’t be long.”

“Okay.” He stared at her for a moment, then gestured to the twins. “Kathleen, grab your doll and whatever else you want to take and meet us in the yard. Kagan, you’re with me.”

The twins got up, and chairs scraped on the floor. Seamus’s tread was heavy as he walked across the room. The door closed behind him and Kagan with a thud. Kathleen trotted to her bedroom.

Madeline pumped water into the sink, then leaned on the counter, head drooping. When would the awkwardness cease? Seamus had been jovial with the children, but his interaction with her was polite and clinical. What would he say during the forthcoming discussion? Did he regret their marriage? Would he explain that he was in love with the woman in blue? Tears pricked the backs of her eyes. Phoebe would say she was borrowing trouble, but better to be prepared for the worst. That way perhaps the hurt wouldn’t slice quite as deep.

Chapter Fourteen

The ever-present odor of dirt, manure, and animals permeated the air as Madeline plodded beside Seamus toward the small pond at the far end of his property. In front of them, the twins skipped and danced across the pasture. A speck in the distance, Conor waved at them from the barnyard where he was shoeing a horse. Another task she'd taken for granted. There was no end to the skills these men possessed. Yet it was all she could do to put a meal on the table and mend their clothes.

She swallowed a sigh and nibbled on her lower lip. Perspiration slicked her palms. After they reached their destination, the dreaded conversation would take place. A conversation sure to dash the little hope she had when she arrived. Was her sister correct that moving West as a mail-order bride—a proxy bride to boot—was a poor decision?

But her choices had been limited—correction—nonexistent. With no home, no marriage prospects, and no abilities to speak of, she was reduced to marrying a man she'd never met and traveling hundreds of miles to raise children and care for his brother. Despite their differences, Seamus seemed to be a good, hardworking man. Not the layabout her father claimed typified the Irish.

The breeze tickled her cheeks and tugged at the pins in her hair. Did the wind ever stop blowing across the plains? Would she ever be able to sit on the porch and enjoy a day that was quiet and still? What would winter be like? She shivered. How much snow would blanket their surroundings? Would she be trapped in the house for months on end?

Visions of Seamus sitting by the fire floated through her mind. The red-orange glow flickering on his angular face, his green eyes sparkling in the light from the flames. His shirt stretched tight on his shoulders as he crossed his arms.

Her mouth dried, and she licked her lips. She had no right to ruminate on his handsome features. He cared for someone else. She would have to create her own happiness with the children.

"A penny for your thoughts." Seamus's voice broke the silence.

Face warm, her gaze shot to his face. "Just thinking about Kagan and Kathleen."

He seemed to study her. "Only the twins? You've been awfully quiet."

She shrugged. "I'm new to raising children this young. There's a lot to consider. I don't want to presume I know what I'm doing. I don't want to let down Conor or you. You've both put your trust in me."

A shadow darkened his expression for a split second. "You're making an effort. We couldn't ask for more."

What had she said to cause such a look? "Yes, you could. A lot of work is required to keep the farm and house running, to say nothing of educating the children."

"You've only been with us for a couple of weeks. Give yourself some grace and time." He cocked his head and peered at her. "We haven't discussed what's upsetting you. Is it frustration with the kids or with me? Have I done something to offend you?"

The woman in blue edged into Madeline's mind, and she shook her head. "No. Nothing. I want to do right by you. That's all."

They arrived at the pond, and Kagan ran to the edge of the water. "Uncle Seamus, I see fish! Come quick and bring the poles."

Seamus chuckled. "The child has quite an imagination. There are no fish in our little body of water, so I'm not sure what he's looking at."

Wide eyed, Madeline gaped at him. "You're lying to him? Letting him think there are fish to be caught?"

"What?" His face flamed. "No. I've told him countless times there's nothing to be had here, but he insists I'm wrong."

"Perhaps he's seeing tadpoles. They can look like fish to the untrained."

"I never thought of frogs." He beamed at her. "Brilliant. Let's prove your hypothesis." He caught her elbow and led her toward the little boy squatting on the grass.

"What's a tadpole?" Kathleen stood behind them, her face scrunched in confusion. "And how do you know about them?"

"The tadpole a baby frog and is also called a pollywog. When I was little, about your age, actually, we went to the Berkshire Mountains in Massachusetts with friends. We stayed in their summer home on a lake. Their son loved frogs, so he talked about them incessantly." A shudder wracked her spine. "And he would put them in his pockets and bring them out at the most...inopportune time."

"Like when a certain little girl wasn't expecting it?" Seamus smiled, and his eyes crinkled at the edges.

Her pulse quickened, and her lips curved. Why did he have be so handsome? "Yes. He was a scamp. But he never lost his love of them, and is now a biology professor at one of the universities in Boston."

They knelt next to Kagan who pointed at the small globules sporting tails and feathery external gills. Darting through the water, they appeared as sleek fish, so the child's assumption was understandable. She patted Kagan on the back. "I'm sorry, but these aren't fish. They are going to grow up to be frogs."

His eyes bulged. "Frogs? Can I have one?"

Madeline swallowed a grin. Shades of her childhood friend. "They must stay in the water to survive. But we can come here as often as you'd like to watch them develop." She slid her gaze toward Seamus. "And then you may write a report on what you learned."

"I can do that. How long before they are frogs?" His excitement was palpable. "Can we come every day?"

"No." Kathleen shook her head. "We don't want to see dumb tadthingies every day."

"You don't need to join us, Kathleen. We'll find something you enjoy." Madeline turned back to Kagan. "But no school today, so we'll talk about them tomorrow. How's that sound?"

"Okay, Miss Madeline."

"Ho!" Conor's shout floated across the breeze.

"Daddy. Come see the baby frogs." Kagan jumped up and gestured to his father.

Conor trotted toward them, a broad smile on his face.

"Enough about amphibians for me. Conor can take over. Let's sit under the trees." Seamus climbed to his feet, then grabbed her hands and helped her rise.

Her fingers sizzled in his grasp, and she sucked in a breath. Once she gained her balance, she tucked her hands into the folds of her skirt. Did he feel anything when they touched? She followed him to the copse of pin oaks where he laid out the blanket he'd dropped on their arrival. The shade dropped the temperature several degrees. She leaned against one of the trunks, and Seamus sat at the edge of the cloth.

"I brought *The Innocents* by Mark Twain." He pulled a slim volume from his jacket pocket and winked. "It's not *Little Women* or Ralph Waldo Emerson, but I think you'll enjoy it. How about if I read to us?"

"T-that would be lovely," she stuttered.

He opened the book and began to read, the inflection of his voice changing as he recited the dialogue. Would he never cease surprising her? Didn't he want to discuss what happened on the way home from church? He loved the woman in blue. Why was he being so nice? Madeline peeked at his face, and her stomach clenched. He would never want a real relationship with her, would he?

Chapter Fifteen

The wind ruffled the pages of the book in Seamus's hand. He glanced at Madeline reclined against the trunk of the tree, the dappled sunlight through the branches casting shadows across her face. Eyes closed, her breathing was deep and even. Had she fallen asleep? Had he bored her with his book selection?

An errant lock of hair blew across her cheeks, and he stifled the desire to tuck the stand behind her ear. They'd had few conversations about the nature of their marital relationship and what lay ahead. Would she ever care for him as a wife for her husband? Why would she? He'd saddled her with the care of two children, a brother with deep-seated emotional problems, and back-breaking work.

Her porcelain skin looked soft, and the worry lines she often wore had smoothed. She was a beautiful woman, and a sweet, gentle soul. What had he done to deserve her? *Thank You, Lord, for sending her to us.*

She sighed, and her eyes opened, glazed at first, then clear with intelligence and wit. She pinked and brushed her cheeks. "You're staring. Do I have something on my face?"

He blinked. He'd been caught gaping at her like a schoolboy. "No. It seemed as if you fell asleep. I was trying to decide whether or not to continue reading." He cocked his head. "Would you like a break? Perhaps a walk around the pond?"

"It was rude of me to doze. I didn't think I was tired, but the breeze, the shade...it wasn't you. I enjoyed the story, but a walk would be nice. Get the blood flowing, you know."

"You've nothing to be embarrassed about. We've worked you hard." He smiled. "You deserve a nap." He closed the book and laid it on the blanket, then stood and held out his hand. She clutched his fingers and pulled herself to her feet. His palm sizzled in her touch.

Releasing her grasp, she crossed her arms and turned to Kathleen who sat cross-legged on the ground murmuring to her doll. "Would you like to take a walk with Uncle Seamus and me?"

The child looked up and squinted. "Do I have to?"

"Not at all, but I didn't want you to feel left out in case you wanted to go."

She stared at them for a few seconds, then shook her head. "No, I'll stay here."

Stuffing his hands in his pockets, Seamus called out to Kagan. "Madeline and I are going to stroll around the pond. Please move away from the water until we return. Understood?"

He frowned but nodded. "Yes, sir. Will you be long?"

Madeline giggled, a musical sound. "You could go with us."

"No, you'll just talk and that's boring."

"An honest lad, aren't you?" Seamus chuckled. "We'll play tag when we get back."

The boy's face lit up, and he clapped his hands. "And you'll be *It*."

"Deal." He ruffled Kagan's hair and waved at Kathleen who barely gave them a glance. He held out his arm. "The ground may be uneven. Why don't you hold on for safety's sake? Can't have you twisting an ankle."

Her face flamed, and she slipped her hand into the crook of his elbow.

He enjoyed making her blush which happened often. Her hand was warm through his shirtsleeve. He led her past the rushes clustered near the edge of the water. Soon bees would dart among the grassy stalks.

They walked in silence as he considered and discarded possible topics. Anything he thought of seemed mundane for an educated woman of the world like Madeline. All he knew was farming. And war. Definitely not a subject for discussion.

"Do—"

"Th—"

He dipped his head. "You first."

"I was going to thank you for taking the day off. You must have plenty of work to do, even on a Sunday."

"There will always be tasks to complete, but even though the children aren't mine, sometimes it feels as if they are, and they will be grown and gone soon enough. And you and I need to get acquainted. What better way to do that than a picnic?"

She stared across the water at the twins. "They've already changed since my arrival. Kagan seems more sure of himself, and Kathleen...well, she's not quite as..."

"Belligerent?" He quirked one eyebrow.

"Let's say challenging." A gentle smile tugged at her lips. "I believe she may be starting to trust me."

"As well she should."

"Easy to say. Difficult to do. She's had a lot of hurts in her short life. Give her time."

"How did you become so patient and wise?"

Her lips pressed into a slash, and she shrugged.

He patted her hand. "I've upset you."

"No. Sometimes the Lord teaches us patience and wisdom through adversity, and it still aches to think of it, but now I'm here, in a better place. So, we'll forget the past and enjoy the present. Like playing a game of tag."

"Do you really want to do that?" He studied her expression.

"Absolutely. I'm not very good at it, but it will be fun nonetheless."

They rounded the pond, and Kagan raced toward them, arms flailing. "You're back! That wasn't too long, especially since I could see you. If I couldn't, then I would wonder how much more until you would come." He tugged at Madeline's hand. "Have you ever played tag before? I could teach you."

Conor stood near the shore, hands in his pockets. "You're in for it now, Madeline. Tag is his favorite pastime."

Seamus bent and lifted Kagan above his head. "Take a breath, little man."

Kagan squealed. "Swing me, Uncle Seamus."

"Then I'll be too tired for tag."

"Then I'll win." The boy grinned and squirmed.

Setting down the child, Seamus glanced at Madeline who watched the exchange with a wide smile.

Kathleen rolled her eyes. "Are we going to play tag or just talk about it?"

"Be nice, young lady." Seamus tugged at her hair. "Now, if I remember correctly, I'm It, so I'll count to three before I come after you. One. Two. Three!"

The kids and Conor took off in opposite directions, and Madeline ran for the trees. Seamus trotted toward Kagan, then pretended to lose his footing. The youngster spun and rushed toward his sister. Arms outstretched, Seamus followed him. Behind him, the silvery tones of Madeline's giggle carried on the breeze.

He whirled and bolted toward her, his legs eating up the distance between them. She shrieked and pivoted, but he was too fast. Before he could regret the decision, he scooped her up, then swung her over his shoulder. She pounded on his back, and he guffawed. "Thought you could get away from me?"

"You're It, Miss Madeline." Kagan applauded.

Sucking in air, Seamus put her down. How would she react to his spontaneous action?

Madeline's foot caught in her skirt, and she staggered.

He seized her arms before she could fall, and she stumbled against him, the scent of her soap wafting into his nose. His throat tightened. Heart thundering in his chest, he looked down at her. Their faces were inches apart.

Cheeks flushed, her face had a thin sheen of perspiration, giving her an ethereal glow. Her pupils dilated, and her lips parted. Dare he kiss her?

Chapter Sixteen

Trembling, Madeline stared up at Seamus. His green eyes darkened as he seemed to search her face. He released his grip on her and slid his arms around her, the feel of his hand gentle through the fabric of her dress. Tingles radiated from her back to her belly, and her toes curled. Was he going to kiss her? Did she want him to?

She leaned into him, and his embrace tightened. He lowered his head, and—

"Uncle Seamus!" Kathleen's voice was strident and panic filled.

Startled, Madeline pulled away.

He dropped his hands and whirled. "What is it?"

Bereft of his closeness, she peered around him.

The child darted across the grassy expanse, her arms waving. Tears streamed down her cheeks, her freckles standing out against her ashen face.

A chill washed over Madeline, and she whipped her head back and forth, her gaze searching the property. Her lunch threatened to reappear as nausea roiled in her stomach. Where was Kagan? Had he fallen into the pond?

She pushed passed Seamus and rushed to meet Kathleen. Dropping to her knees, she grabbed her shoulders. "Kagan. Where is Kagan?"

"He's lying next to the pond. It's Daddy. I can't find him." The girl's lower lip quivered. "I ran away from him so Uncle Seamus wouldn't tag me. When I saw he wasn't chasing me, I came back. Then he was hugging you, so I looked for Daddy. And now I can't find him." She wailed and dropped her head on Madeline's shoulder.

Madeline wrapped her in a hug and looked over her head at Seamus. "The pond?" she mouthed.

His eyes widened, and he bent close to the crying child. He stroked her hair. "Where was your dad when you saw him last? Near the water or somewhere else?"

She raised her head and hiccupped. Red rimmed, her eyes took on a distant stare. "Um...not the pond. He was over there." She pointed to the far pasture. "He climbed the fence and went into the field."

Seamus blew out a loud breath. "So he didn't go swimming?"

"No. We were playing tag." Head tilted, her mouth was twisted in a frown. "Why would he go swimming?"

"Right. I thought he might try to hide in the cattails."

Kathleen shook her head and gestured toward the meadow. "He was over there."

"Good girl." He patted her shoulder, then bent and whispered in Madeline's ear. "Because we can't see him in any of the fields, I think he went into the woods. He's always been fascinated with the forest, and last year he wandered inside and got disoriented. Was gone for a couple of hours before I realized it."

Madeline laced her fingers with Kathleen's, then stood. Her vision swirled, and she blinked. She couldn't let the child see how terrified she was that they might never see her father again. *Please, God, no.* Stiffening her spine, she captured Seamus's hand. "I know time is of the essence, but please pray. God is watching over him and will guide us."

"I should have thought of that. Thank you for the reminder that He's in control." Seamus squeezed her hand, then completed the circle by clasping Kathleen's fingers in his own. "Dear heavenly Father, we're scared for Conor. We love him and don't want to lose him. You love him even more than we do." His voice broke, and he cleared his throat. "Please keep him safe, and help us find him. In the name of Your Son, Jesus, amen." He palmed moisture from his eyes. "Okay, Katie-girl. Collect your brother, and we'll go look for your father."

She nodded and wrapped her arms around his knees in a quick embrace. "Don't worry, Uncle Seamus. God will help you find him." She waved and scampered toward Kagan.

"The faith of a little child." A frown creased Seamus's forehead. "I wish I had as much."

"You do, or you wouldn't have prayed." She picked up her skirts and began to jog toward the woods, Seamus by her side. The children caught up with them and followed them to the trees.

A lump formed in her throat. *Forgive me, Father. I should have been paying closer attention to the children and their dad. It's my fault Conor is missing. Please don't let him be injured on my account. Help us find him.*

Breath ragged and loud, she swiped away the tears that had formed. She entered the tangle of trees behind Seamus and shouted, "Conor, where are you?"

Ears straining, she listened for a response.

Nothing.

Her chest heaved with exertion, and she called out again. "Conor."

"Conor." Seamus's deep voice boomed in the dimness.

She didn't deserve this family. Intent on Seamus's closeness, his embrace, his impending kiss, she'd lost sight of the others. And now Conor was lost. Guilt warred with disappointment. What would Seamus's lips have felt like pressed onto hers? His embrace had been gentle but firm. Would his kiss have been the same? Her face heated, and her pulse skipped. She must focus on finding the Conor not relive a kiss that didn't happen.

When Seamus came to his senses after this was over, he'd realize she wasn't fit to help raise the twins or care for his brother. Her life of tea parties and embroidering samplers had ill-prepared her for rearing youngsters or caring for a man with mental problems.

A sob broke loose, and she clamped her lips.

"We'll find him." Seamus stopped her with a hand on her arm.

Her arm tingled under his touch. "But will he be okay?"

"I got into my fair share of scrapes as a lad, and I turned out fine." A reassuring smile clung to his mouth. "It's not been long enough for him to go far."

"But he could have gone in any direction."

"True, but God will guide us."

Her stomach hollowed. Now whose faith was faltering? She nodded, her body heavy. Seamus was a good man. Encouraging her at every turn. Kind despite her shortcomings. Gracious in the face of Conor's disappearance, holding her blameless. God had shown her compassion by providing a righteous and considerate husband. A man who was slowly tunneling his way into her heart. Would he ever care for her?

The image of the woman in blue pushed its way into her mind, and Madeline nearly fell to her knees. In the joy of the afternoon, she'd forgotten about the incident at church. The shared smiles between Seamus and the woman. Her hand on his arm with familiarity.

Pain knifed Madeline. Theirs was a marriage of convenience. She must never forget his heart belonged to another.

Chapter Seventeen

They pushed their way through the underbrush, Kathleen and Kagan thrashing at the bushes.

"Conor," Seamus hollered.

"Daddy," Kathleen's shrill cry cut through the birdsong.

"Hello?" Conor's muffled voice sounded from the east.

Stomach flipping, Seamus jerked his head toward the call. His brother was alive and sounded as if he was okay. At least well enough to respond to their calls. "Conor." He rushed in the direction of his brother's voice, Madeline and the children close behind him. "We're coming, Conor."

He entered a small clearing.

Conor sat on a fallen tree, his hands wrapped around his middle, relief etched on his face. He appeared uninjured.

Seamus knelt in front of his brother, then ran his hands over Conor's arms and legs. "Are you hurt? How do you feel?"

"Not hurt, just embarrassed. I got lost. I know I'm not supposed to come into the woods alone, but it was hot, and I knew it would be cooler under the trees. Then I saw a rabbit and decided to try catching it for dinner." He shrugged. "So I looked for branches to make the trap and wandered too far. By the time I realized what had happened, I had no idea where I was."

Seamus rose and walked toward Madeline, hands shoved into his pockets. Yelling at his brother would only upset everyone, but the man deserved a tongue-lashing for worrying them.

Grace, my Son. Show him grace.

Face warm, Seamus ducked his head.

Kathleen ran forward and hugged Conor. "We were worried, Daddy."

He embraced his daughter. "I know, honey. Daddy was foolish again. Forgive me?"

Her face lit up, and she kissed his cheek. "Always." She grasped his hand and tugged. "We have to go. I left my doll on the blanket."

Conor chuckled. "Then by all means, we must hurry. She'll be afraid by herself." He held out his other hand, and Kagan grabbed it.

"This way." Seamus gestured in the direction for them to retrace their steps.

"Were you afraid, Daddy?" Kagan's voice quavered.

"No, I knew Madeline would come for me. She always does."

"Yes. She's good that way," said Kagan.

Seamus exchanged a glance with her, and Madeline shook her head, her face flushed. Conor's trust in her was well placed. She might not have been able to track his brother, but her suggestion to pray and give their plight to the Lord was the best decision for all involved. He studied her from under the brim of his hat.

He'd been wrong to be disappointed when she arrived. Assumptions and expectations had colored his attitude. As a believer, he trusted that God has selected and prepared his wife for him, yet he'd been discontented on and off since Madeline appeared. Life would not be as sweet without her. *Forgive me, God. I'm a selfish and ungrateful man.*

They emerged from the woods, and Seamus blinked against the glare. His chest lightened. The danger had passed, and Conor was safe. He rubbed his hands together. "I guess tag is out of the question, but how about if we play blindman's buff?"

"No, we need to get Conor back to the house." Madeline laid her hand on Seamus's arm. "He could be dehydrated."

"You're not thirsty, are you, Daddy?" Kathleen peered at Conor.

"Maybe a little bit."

"But we want to stay and play. Can you go the house by yourself?" Kagan gestured to the small basin. "Or get water from the pond?"

"Children, it's important that we all go home."

"But he's not thirsty." Kathleen wore a mulish expression.

Seamus held up his hands. "We're done for the day. Do what Madeline says." He leaned close to Madeline and whispered, "Are you sure?"

She gave him a curt nod. “Yes, not only for physical reasons, but he could suffer an episode. Unlikely, because he wasn’t disoriented when we found him, but let’s not risk the possibility.”

He straightened. “Of course. I didn’t think of that.”

Kathleen stomped her foot. “It’s not fair. Just because he was lost for a little while. He’s found, so why do we have to be done?”

“I am tired, Daughter.” Conor rubbed his forehead. “Please don’t argue or talk about me as if I can’t hear you.”

The girl’s lip trembled, and she opened her mouth as if to say something, then clamped it shut and ran toward the cabin.

“Kathleen, wait.” Kagan raced after her.

Shoulders slumped, Conor trudged in their wake.

Madeline hastened to his side and looped her arm with his. “Conor, I’m sorry for how the children acted. Please don’t be troubled. God loves you just as you are. You are a special person, made in His image, and we are here to help Him take care of you.”

“But I’m damaged. I’m not like Him.”

“We’re all damaged, Conor. Not in the same way, but broken nonetheless. That’s why Jesus came. To heal our fractured hearts and souls. It’s hard to remember that when others remind us of our problems. I’ll speak to the children.”

“No, I will do that, Madeline.” A weary smile hovered on his lips. “Thank you for your kind words. I’m glad you’re part of our family. My brother did a wonderful thing by marrying you. Would you and Seamus give me some time with the twins?"

"Absolutely." She patted his hand. "I'll be praying for you."

Conor kissed her cheek and picked up his pace as he continued toward the house.

She tucked her hands in her pockets as Seamus drew next to her. He nudged her shoulder. "Your wisdom continues to humble me."

Her cheeks pinked, and she dropped her gaze. "Wisdom is the last word I'd use to describe myself. I stumble through each day, like those newborn calves, barely able to keep my feet under me."

"I hate that you feel that way because you challenge me and make me consider things in a different way." He tugged at the brim of his hat. "In my frustration with Conor and the difficulties his problems cause, I've failed to see him as God's child, to recognize his specialness. Most of the time, he's just one more issue I have to handle. He's my brother, and I love him, but I often don't like him. In fact, I resent him and how much harder our lives are because of his condition."

"Understandable. It was like that with my sisters. I will pray for your feelings to change. Only God can help us in our relationships to others."

"See? Wisdom. I'm a terrible, selfish man." His throat thickened, and he swallowed.

"You're human, like the rest of us. You've been dealing with your brother's condition for years. Alone. But I'm here to lighten your burden.

And now you can focus on the farm without worrying what's happening with him or the children. I'm pleased to be able to help." Her face reddened. "And I promise to get better at the household tasks."

Seamus stuffed his hands into his pockets. She was pleased. Would her feelings ever run more deeply than satisfaction? Could she ever feel something for him, or would their life together always be about his brother?

Chapter Eighteen

Madeline dunked the cook pot into the sudsy water and scrubbed at the stubborn bits of food clinging to the metal. The twins were in bed, and the men had gone to the barn to take care of the animals. A never-ending chore. She blew an errant strand of hair out of her face. Perspiration trickled down her back. Unseasonably hot temperatures created a hot and sticky night, and no breeze brought relief through the open window.

The oven continued to push heat into the room. Perhaps making a pot roast hadn't been the wisest decision, but when Seamus let slip that the hearty dish made with pork was his favorite meal, she couldn't resist making the dish. He worked long hours, and his patience with her knew no bounds. The least she could do was prepare food he loved.

Nearly a week had passed since they'd had to hunt for Conor in the woods. A week of blessed routine. The children had done their schoolwork without question each morning, and twice Kathleen accompanied them to the pond to check the progress of the tadpoles. The child's adversarial behavior was diminishing, with fewer arguments arising. She'd shown artistic abilities beyond her age with a pencil sketch capturing the image of her brother squatting at the water's edge, his delight at the wonders of nature evident by a broad grin.

After dinner each night, Conor would play checkers or jacks with the twins, and Seamus would read aloud. She occasionally joined in, but games had never been her forte, so she preferred to immerse herself in the sound of his soothing, bass voice rising and falling. The stories came alive, and she lost herself in the words.

As promised, Seamus had tilled the vegetable garden, and he'd also cleared away grass and scrub from the front of the cabin, so Madeline could plant flowers when the weather improved. She'd spent hours with the Montgomery Ward catalog, then he'd surprised her taking her to the general store where a full selection hung ready for purchase. They'd returned from the trip, and he dragged out wooden boxes from the barn and filled them with dirt to give her a place to start seedlings.

Working side by side to complete the task, they bumped shoulders and grazed hands. Her pulse skittered, and her skin tingled at the memory. She bent over the pot with more vigor. Mooning over the man would do her no good. He treated her with kindness, nothing more. He'd complimented her on tonight's dinner, but his face remained somber through most of the meal.

Her cooking had improved with practice, but maybe her rendition of his favorite food wasn't as delicious as he was used to. Had he praised her out of habit or good manners? Had the meal dredged up the grief of losing his parents because of memories the dish provoked? She rinsed the pot and propped it on a towel beside the sink. Were her attempts to make Seamus happy futile?

She glanced at the watch pinned to her bodice. He and his brother would be in the barn for at least another thirty minutes. She dried the pot, drained the sink, and wiped down the counters and table. The children had put away their toys and schoolbooks, so the only chore remaining was to work on the dress she'd begun for Kathleen.

Years of stitching samplers had given Madeline the ability to make small, even stitches, but figuring out how to assemble the parts of the outfit had caused more than a few hours of frustration and rework. Would the child outgrow the clothing before she could finish it?

Madeline lit the lamp on the table by the rocker and dropped into the chair, then bent to retrieve the garment from the basket. The lavender floral fabric was soft under her fingers and would highlight Kathleen's sapphire eyes. A cute little girl, she'd be a gorgeous woman when fully grown. Seamus and Conor would have their work cut out for them when suitors began to come calling.

The sound of crickets wafted into the room from outside, a noise barely discernable in the streets of downtown Boston. She peered into the night and smiled at the dots of light that flickered in the darkness as fireflies sought their mates. If only marriage was that easy.

Bending over the dress, Madeline blinked back tears. Seamus still bunked with Conor and hadn't raised the topic of moving into the house. Would he sleep in the barn for the rest of their lives? Did he not find her marginally attractive? Her face flamed. Far be it for her to introduce the subject, but it hurt that he didn't seem interested in consummating their marriage. Would simple friendship be her lot?

She nibbled her lower lip and slipped the needle through the edge of the dress. "Forgive me, Father. I'm being ungrateful again. You provided a solution to a difficult problem, and I have a family now. One in which I don't have to be afraid or feel condescension. I was too young when Mother died to know how she and Father felt about each other, but he grieved her loss as if they loved one another. Is it too much to ask for the love of my husband? Or do You want to me to learn contentment in the camaraderie Seamus and I have?"

A sharp prick of pain stabbed her finger, and she gasped. A drop of blood appeared and oozed onto the fabric, and her eyes welled. Now she'd ruined the garment. Was there no end to her ineptitude? Tears coursed down her cheeks, and she fumbled for her handkerchief.

The woman in blue had to be a better choice as Seamus's wife. She was attractive, dressed well, and could probably tackle every household chore with grace and efficiency. And most of all, Seamus seemed to care for her. If Madeline had their marriage annulled, then he could marry the woman with no impediments.

Her stomach clenched. She'd miss them, even contrary Kathleen. Would they miss her, or would the memory of her short stay with them fade into obscurity? Perhaps that was best. She was the interloper, the one who'd upset their well-ordered lives with her inabilities.

She would inform Seamus of her decision as soon as he entered the house. Her lips trembled. It would be painful to leave, but the right thing to do. Her heart would recover. Wouldn't it?

##

Whistling, Seamus loosened the lid on the crate that held the books he'd ordered for Madeline. He couldn't wait to see her face, the delighted smile that would light up her face when she saw the collection. He was familiar with many of the titles and authors, but Ida had secured a few he'd never heard of. The purchase had been expensive but would be worth the joy it would bring his wife.

His wife.

The words rolled off his tongue. Thus far, they were married in name only. He wanted to give her time to get used to the idea of being married but to also feel some level of affection for him. Would she ever grow to love him? She seemed to enjoy his company and was no longer as skittish as a long-tailed cat in a room full of rocking chairs. Their conversations at dinner were a mixture of frivolity and discussion. She was versed on any number of topics, her opinion a fresh perspective. Initially, she'd balked at sharing her viewpoint, probably a holdover from her home life.

Her eyes sparked with intelligence, and she encouraged the twins to voice their thoughts as well, so even at their age they became used to participating in conversations. Conor often watched rather than talked, but his expression of peace spoke volumes.

A month had passed since her arrival, yet Madeline had changed their lives as if she'd been with them for years. Kagan was confident, and Kathleen had softened tremendously. Both children had made significant progress in their studies, nearly catching up to where they should be. Conor hadn't had any incidents since returning from the woods. He could at any time, but the atmosphere of tranquility seemed to keep him from getting agitated.

Would she allow him to read to her from one of her new books, or would she want to savor them alone in the privacy of her room? Thoughts of her seated near the fire, the orange glow flickering on her cheeks and glinting off her auburn hair consumed him. What would it be like to release her gleaming, cinnamon-colored hair from the bun at the base of her head? Would it feel as silky as it appeared?

His heart thumped wildly, and he pressed his hand against his chest. Slow down, boy. You don't know how she feels. Forcing your attentions on her would be bad form. He blew out a breath. Not unlike breaking a horse, he needed to take his time, guiding her to accept him. Would his gift be one step closer to that possibility?

Seamus tossed the hammer on the bench and hefted the crate onto his shoulder. As the adage said, there was no time like the present. He hurried from the barn to the house. With a quick twist of the knob, he opened the door, and stepped inside. "I've got—"

Madeline sat in the chair by the window, a pile of floral fabric in her lap. She cradled one hand, and her face was damp with tears.

He set down the crate with a thump, then rushed over and knelt beside her. "What's wrong?" He drew her hand into his and inspected it. "Are you injured? I could go for the doctor."

She pulled her fingers out of his palm and wrapped her arms around her middle. "Just a pinprick, nothing more."

"Then why are you so upset? Did the kids say something hurtful? Conor? Is he all right?"

"He's fine, and the twins are asleep." She swiped at the moisture on her face. Her shoulders were hunched, and she refused to meet his gaze.

"I don't understand." His stomach hollowed. Just when he thought they'd reached an equilibrium.

"I'm sorry for not being able to make you happy. I've tried my best, but I keep messing up." She sniffled and held up the fabric. "I can't sew a simple dress for Kathleen, and dinner tonight was an abysmal failure. You deserve someone much more suited to farm life...and to you."

His eyes widened, and he took the garment from her, then set in the basket. What was she saying? "Dinner was delicious, just like my mother used to make, and as far as clothing goes, we can have one of the women in town make her outfits."

"Your face. You looked...I don't know...somber."

"I was, for a fleeting moment. Like I said, the dish reminded me of Ma, and it made me miss her, but in a good way. Reminding me of good times with her." He took her hand again, and this time she didn't pull away. "You are the best thing to happen to our family in a very long time. You can't expect to know how to do everything in a few weeks."

"But what about the woman at church? Aren't you in love with her? I saw you two...talking...laughing...touching. Why didn't you marry her?"

"Who?"

"A brown-haired lady wearing a bright blue dress and hat. The two of you stood on the church steps for a while. She kept her hand on your arm a very long time. You seemed...close, and I shouldn't stand in the way of true love. You should be free to marry whomever you wish." Tears slipped from the corners of her eyes, and her lip quivered. "I'm willing to bow out and seek an annulment. I'm sure I can find a job somewhere. Perhaps a lady's companion—"

Seamus pressed his fingers against her mouth. "Stop. First of all, the woman I was speaking with is Ida Weber, widowed when her husband died a couple of years ago. Even if she was interested in me, which she is not, I do not, nor did I ever, love her. She is a good friend, as close as a sister, but nothing more. You are my wife, which pleases me greatly. But I've apparently done a terrible job of showing you."

Madeline tried to speak.

"Hush." He winked. "I'm not finished. Secondly, the reason I was talking to her was to make arrangements for your gift." He jerked his head at the abandoned crate. "She is starting a lending library here in town, and she helped me make selections for you."

"Gift?" Her gaze darted from his face to the wooden box, curiosity warring with disbelief.

"Yes." He thumbed the wetness from her cheeks, then grabbed her hand to help her from the chair. "I wanted to help you get adjusted here. I'm sure you miss the culture and opportunities of Boston, and you seemed to enjoy our reading, so I secured a few books for you."

"Books?" Her face lit up, and she dragged him across the room.

His chest swelled. Success. He'd made the right choice. With a flourish, he yanked the lid off the crate and stepped back.

"Oh, Seamus. They're wonderful." One by one she pulled out the volumes, stroking the spines as she mouthed the titles. "I don't know which one to read first." Her face pink, she gave him a shy smile. "Would you like to decide?"

"But they're your present. You should pick."

"What if you don't like my choice?"

"Not possible." He grinned like a possum eating a sweet potato. "Does that mean we're going to read the book together?"

Her color deepened. "I'd like that, if you don't mind."

"Mind? Nothing would make me happier." He tilted his head and wrinkled his forehead in an exaggerated frown. "Hmmm. Which one?" He rubbed his jaw. "How about *Lorna Doone?* I always like romance."

She giggled, but seconds later her laughter turned to tears.

Seamus stared at her. Would he ever understand this woman to whom he was married?

Chapter Nineteen

"I hate arithmetic."

Madeline looked up from her sewing as Kagan threw down his pencil, his face twisted into a frown. She laid down the garment and went to the table where she sat in the chair next to him. She laid her hand on his. "You want to know a secret?"

His gaze shot to her face. "Yes, anything but this."

She put her mouth close to his ear and whispered, "I don't like math either."

He lit up. "You don't?"

"No. I'd much rather read a book. I love words. Numbers, not so much."

"Then why are you making us learn about them? We don't have to, you know."

A giggle bubbled up, and she shook her head. "But we do. With your love of animals and the outside world, it seems like you might be a farmer like your dad and uncle."

"Do they know arithmetic?" Doubt colored Kagan's words, and he glanced at the door as if expecting the men to walk into the house.

"They do, and can you figure out why the skill is necessary?"

He shrugged and fiddled with the pencil.

"Because they need to know how many cows and horses they have, or how many eggs we've collected, or most importantly, how to count money."

Kagan's eyes widened, and he nodded. "I've seen him pay for things at the store, but I didn't think about what that meant."

"So you understand why you need to at least learn the basics."

"Yes, ma'am. But I don't have to like it, right?"

"No." She ruffled his hair. "How about if you take a break? Draw me a picture of what the tadpoles looked like the last time you visited the pond."

"Almost like frogs." He wiped off his slate.

"They look weird if you ask me." Kathleen glanced up from working on a sampler and shuddered. "Why did God make them like that?"

"A very good question, but I'm afraid I don't have an answer."

Kathleen studied her for a moment, then nodded and dropped her attention to the stitching in her lap.

Madeline exhaled. The child was still not shy about giving her opinion, but she hadn't made fun of her brother or criticized Madeline's response. More progress. She rose and went back to her sewing. Should she tell Kagan she didn't like this chore either?

Using her toe to rock the chair, she looked out the window. Seamus had introduced her to Johanna Brennan, the woman at the next farm, who'd also come West as a mail-order bride. From Chicago, she hadn't known how to do many of the skills required of a farmer's wife when she'd arrived two years ago.

Now, as proficient as if she'd been here her whole life, she'd come over on several occasions to help Madeline. Working together, they'd made a shirt and a pair of pants for Kagan, finished Kathleen's dress, and started a shirt for Seamus. Johanna had also shown her several quick and easy recipes, so dinner no longer took all afternoon to prepare. With a great deal of laughter, the woman regaled her with stories of her own mistakes.

Madeline's gaze swept the landscape outside, but there was no movement. Seamus and Conor had headed to the far pasture first thing, taking their midday meal with them, so they wouldn't be back until late afternoon. That knowledge did little to ease her disappointment at their absence, especially Seamus. The room was empty without him.

Not that he was loud or boisterous, and he wasn't even as tall or broad as his brother, but when he was inside, he filled the room. Conversation, laughter, and his smooth, deep voice as he read aloud. The soothing sound of his words made her want to curl up in his lap and lay her head on his chest. Her face warmed. Did that make her a wanton woman?

Seamus's familiar whistle wafted in through the open window, and her heart skipped. She searched the yard. He appeared around the corner of the barn and strode toward the house. Why was he home early?

She patted her hair, then tucked her sewing in the basket and flattened the wrinkles from her skirt. Pulse racing, she rose and hurried to the door.

His steps sounded on the porch, then the door swung open. He stood on the threshold, his green eyes twinkling above his deeply tanned cheeks. He pulled off his hat, and his hair stuck to his head with perspiration. His gaze ricocheted around the room until it came to rest on her face. A smile tugged at his lips. "Time for the kids' riding lessons. Can I steal them away?"

The twins leapt up and raced toward Seamus.

Breathless, she nodded. "Certainly." She tore her eyes from his to look at the twins. "But they need to put away their things before they go."

"Of course."

Frowning, Kathleen and Kagan hurried to where they'd been working, grabbed their stuff, and ran into their room. Seconds later, they returned, no doubt having tossed the items onto their beds.

"Have a good time." She tugged at her collar. "When can I expect you for dinner?"

"You can't because you're going, too." Seamus smirked. "It's about time for you to learn to ride as well."

"Oh, I don't—"

"Yay! Come on, Miss Madeline." Kagan clapped his hands. "It will be fun."

"You heard the boy. I happen to know there is a split skirt in the bottom of that trunk that should fit you. You've got five minutes." He winked. "We'll be outside."

"But—"

"No excuses. I knew if I'd given you fair warning this morning, you'd have come up with all kinds of reasons why you can't go with us."

He waved, put an arm around each child, and led them from the house, his chuckle sending shivers down her spine.

Mouth agape, she stared at the door. How would he know her dress size? Her face scorched. He'd obviously studied her form. And he'd teased her. Was he beginning to care for her? Because she knew without question, she cared for him. More than a little.

##

The front door opened, and Seamus sucked in his breath. Madeline stepped onto the porch, looking gorgeous in the burgundy split skirt and matching jacket. Her expression was slightly less than terrified. He stifled the urge to rub his hands together. Instead, he bowed. "You look lovely. I thought Tillie's skirt might fit you."

"Won't Conor mind seeing me in it?"

"No, besides he headed over to the Brennans' place. They needed a hand with some planting."

"Shouldn't you be over there also? Surely, our lessons can wait."

"Trying to skip school?"

Her face turned a delightful shade of pink, and her eyelashes swept her cheeks as she ducked her head. "No."

"Hmmm. I'm not convinced."

"I've never ridden. It's yet one more thing I don't know how to do." Her voice quavered. "We lost all our horses except a poor old mare during the war, and Father was never able to replace them."

"Then it's not your fault you can't ride, and it will be my pleasure to teach you." He held out his arm. "May I escort you to the barn?"

She curtsied and slipped her hand in the crook of his elbow. "You may, sir." She gripped his arm as if it were a lifeline.

His skin sizzled, and he nearly stumbled. Schooling his features, he patted her hand, then regretted the action when his palm tingled. He cleared his throat. "You're going to do fine. This is the kids' first lesson, so it's perfect timing to start you as well. The horses we'll ride will be much like your poor old mare. Strong, but they've seen a lifetime of work, so we don't use them for much anymore. You'll be on Buttercup. How scary can a horse be with that name?"

"I'll wait until I see how big she is." She gave him a saucy grin. "Then I'll let you know."

He threw his head back and roared with laughter. Madeline had pluck; he'd give her that. "Fair enough." They entered the barn, and he led her to the nearest stall.

The twins jumped up from the bale of hay and ran to them. Kagan tugged at Seamus's coat. "When can we start? I want to go riding."

"There's quite a bit to learn before you climb on an animal, Kagan. First, you need to meet your horse and learn about him or her: their senses, abilities, and how they communicate."

"You're silly, Uncle Seamus; horses can't talk." The little boy wrinkled his nose.

"Ah, but they can, especially with their bodies." Seamus gestured to the tack hanging on the wall. "Then I'll teach you about the equipment and how to care for your horse."

Kathleen stood with her fists on her hips. "Do we have to know all that before we can ride?"

"No. I'll mix it up, otherwise it would be too boring."

Her eyes widened.

"Yes, I knew what was behind your question." He glanced at Madeline who stood frozen about ten feet from the stall. "But today, we're not going to do any riding, but we will mount the horses to get a feel for what it's like. We'll save riding for tomorrow."

"Awww." Kagan stomped his foot.

Seamus lifted his eyebrow. "Or we could go back inside, and find some chores for you to do."

"Sorry." The little boy looked contrite.

"I know you're disappointed, but it will give you something to look forward to. You'll be riding Brownie, and Socks is Kathleen's pony.

We'll meet them one at a time." He ducked into the stall across the aisle and led Brownie to the doorway that was blocked with a thick rope.

The animal dipped its head and snuffled Kagan's head. The youngster chortled and rubbed his hair. "That tickles." He reached up, patted the long muzzle, then drew back. "He's soft!"

"And you are very brave."

Kagan lifted his chin, a proud gleam in his eye. "Now, you try, Miss Madeline. He won't hurt you."

Seamus cupped her elbow in his hand. "I'll be beside you the whole time."

She nibbled her lower lip and nodded but remained in place.

"You can't reach him from there."

"Right." She inched forward, arm outstretched. Finally close enough, she touched the horse's forehead with the tips of her fingers. The animal blinked and remained in place. Madeline continued to stroke the area between its eyes, a wide smile lighting up her face.

Seamus's chest tightened at her joyous expression. She was beautiful. "And now you are very brave. I'm proud of you."

She flushed and stepped back.

Kagan hugged her knees. "You did it, Miss Madeline. You did it."

Kathleen nodded and patted Madeline's arm. "Thanks for learning to ride with us, Miss Madeline."

"You're welcome." Her voice broke, and she cleared her throat, meeting Seamus's eyes over the kids' heads.

"I love you, Miss Madeline." Kagan tipped up his head.

"And I love you, Kagan." She bent and hugged him.

The little boy twisted his neck and looked at Seamus. "Don't you love her, too?"

"Of course I do." Seamus gulped. Realization dawned. The words tasted sweet, and he meant what he said, but how would Madeline react to his statement?

Chapter Twenty

Madeline waved at the departing wagon, then rotated her shoulders to ease her bunched muscles. She'd have the house to herself for five or six blessed hours. Seamus was taking Conor to an appointment with his doctor after dropping the twins off at their friend's house. It was tempting to sit on the porch and enjoy her solitude, but she'd saved several chores until no one was underfoot. One last glance at the buckboard, and she wiped her hands on her skirt and headed into the cabin. Being alone would also allow her to think about what had happened during yesterday's horseback riding lesson.

Pressing icy fingers to her warm cheeks, she blew out a sigh. Seamus had agreed with Kagan's assertion that he loved her. Was he being polite as usual? Avoiding a touchy subject with his nephew? The man hadn't met her eyes since making the declaration, giving credence to her theory that his words were nothing more than an effort to evade an awkward conversation with Kagan or her.

She opened all the windows, allowing the fresh spring breeze to circulate throughout the house. Standing in the middle of the living room, she let her gaze drift around the space. Small but comfortable, each area held well-made but rustic furniture. Nothing like the gleaming, expensive items that had filled her parent's house, although beautiful in their simplicity.

Her heart clenched. First, the nightmare with her father's partner, then trying to fit into Seamus's family hadn't given her time to grieve. A lump formed in her throat, and she swallowed. "Oh, Father, why did you have to die?" Her eyes prickled, and she pressed her lips together. She couldn't allow herself the luxury of mourning. Too much to do and not enough time to do it.

Stiffening her spine, she made quick work of the dishes, then swept and mopped the floor. The exertion had pushed away her somber thoughts. "Thank You, God. It's not good to wallow in misery. I must accept my circumstances and be thankful for all that You've provided: two delightful children, their father, and a husband." Her mouth tripped over the word.

Seamus was still a husband in name only. When would he expect intimacy? He'd laid to rest her fears about the woman in blue...Ida, but his words of love hung in the air like a specter. Yes, he seemed to like her, but did he really love her as he said?

"Stop it, Madeline. You've gone down the rabbit hole again." She brushed the dangling strands of hair away from her face. "You've got a good life here. Now, get to work." She chuckled. "And talking to yourself has got to stop. If Seamus could hear you, he'd think you'd gone daft."

Humming her favorite hymn, she hurried to the barn and grabbed the buckets of whitewash he'd prepared for her. Staggering under the weight of the pails, she trudged back to the house and set them in the kitchen, then returned to the barn for a brush and some cloths to cover the floor. Seamus had offered to help, but she assured him she'd be able to handle the simple chore. She'd seen children whitewashing fences in Boston, so how hard could it be?

Steps light, Madeline hurried back to the house and cleared away the furniture, then laid the sheets over the counters and floor. "Here goes." She dipped the brush into the bucket then painted a wide swath of the concoction onto the wall. Then another. And another. She stood back to study the effect and smiled. What a difference from the dark wood.

The sharp antiseptic smell of the paint tickled her nose. Perhaps she'd ask Seamus to make enough paint to cover the entire inside. The tiny patch she'd completed already brightened the house to say nothing of the clean scent that clung to the air. An hour later, she'd finished and nearly clapped her hands with satisfaction. How long before the paint dried and she could put things in place?

She shrugged and folded the cloths, then piled them by the door. Having used all the paint, she rinsed the buckets at the outside pump, then carried them to the barn. Her shoulders and back ached from the exertion, but the anticipation of Seamus's praise made the discomfort worth it. An image of his tanned face drifted into her mind, his eyes sparkling with delight at her accomplishment. Her breath hitched, but she wouldn't let herself go back to the argument of whether or not he'd ever care for her. "I can't go there."

Instead, she'd make a special dessert. Seamus had agreed on a cold supper since he didn't know when they'd return, but a pie would be a nice treat. She'd finally gotten the hang of making the crust, and Johanna had shown her how to make chess pie, a simple custard pie the whole family loved.

Hurrying into the bedroom, she washed her hands and face and repinned her hair. She went back to the kitchen and tied on an apron, then assembled the ingredients and lit the stove. She glanced at the watch on her bodice. Still a few more hours before everyone returned. Humming again, she tapped her foot in rhythm to the music.

A noise sounded outside, and she startled. Had something happened? Were they home already? No. She hadn't heard the wagon. Had some sort of wild animal come to visit? Seamus had warned her about the occasional bobcat and coyote. Her heart banged in her chest. Would whatever it was try to come inside? Her eyes widened, and she wrapped her arms around her middle.

A chair. She'd shove a chair in front of the door. No. She'd need something heavier. The kitchen table. That would keep any predators out. She rushed to the table and tugged on one end. The furniture scooted a few inches. Another tug. Another few inches. It was taking too long. Worry slithered up her spine. Should she hide in the bedroom? Was she overreacting?

The heavy tread of a footstep on the porch, and then the doorknob rattled. She stifled a scream. That was no animal. Her gaze riveted on the door, she fumbled behind herself for something she could use as a weapon. Her fingers groped on the counter. Wait. She'd moved everything to paint. *Dear God, save me.*

With a squeal, the door opened, and a large, bearded man stood on the threshold. Hair disheveled, his clothes were rumpled and stained. Even from her distance she could smell the sour odor of his unwashed body. His bleary eyes came to rest on her, and a smirk appeared on his face. "Well, what do we have here?"

"Get out." She pulled herself to her full height of five feet seven inches and glared at him. "Get out now."

The intruder snorted an ugly laugh and clomped into the house. "I'm a guest, little lady. Ain't you gonna treat me as such?"

"Guests are invited. And I didn't invite you." Her voice quavered.

"Doesn't sound like you're too sure about that." He moved closer.

She backed up, bumped into the counter, and her heart sank. Trapped. What if she offered him food? Would he leave quietly? "I can make you a meal. Would you like that?"

Swaggering, he circled the table and swiped at her arm. His ragged fingernails tore the fabric and scraped her skin. "You're the only morsel I want."

Chapter Twenty-One

Seamus pulled the wagon to a stop and glanced at the gaping cabin door. His eyebrow shot up. It wasn't like Madeline to leave the door open. An eerie quiet enveloped the yard. The hair on the back of his neck prickled, and he jumped off the wooden bench. He gestured to Conor. "Check the barn for Madeline. I'll look in the house."

Dust puffing in small clouds under his feet, he hurried inside. "Madeline? We're home." The table was askew, and items from the counters were strewn on the floor. His heart banged in his chest. What happened? Where was she? His gaze roved the room. "Madeline!" His voice was sharp. He shoved chairs out of his way as he threaded between pieces of furniture.

Behind the couch the crumpled form of his wife lay on the floor. Her face was pinched and ashen, her clothing torn with scratch marks on the bare shoulder. Her cheek had the beginnings of a bruise. "No!" He dropped to his knees next to her. Was she alive? He pressed his fingertips to her neck. A pulse throbbed, faint and unsteady.

His hands fisted. Her injuries didn't appear to have been inflicted by an animal. The four-legged kind, anyway. This had all the indications a person had been here. His vision clouded, and he swallowed the desire to roar. Was anything broken? He ran his fingers lightly over her arms and legs and blew out a loud sigh. Her limbs seemed intact. He checked her head and discovered a large bump sticky with blood on the back of her skull.

He climbed to his feet, grabbed a discarded towel, and folded it into a bundle. Gently lifting her head, he pressed the material against the wound. How badly was she hurt? Would she awaken or leave them without regaining consciousness.

"Lord, save her, please." His eyes welled with tears. She couldn't die. "Please, Father," he croaked.

Footsteps clattered on the porch, then stopped behind him. "She's not—"

Seamus held up a hand. Conor couldn't see her. Not like this. "Go for Doc Abbott. Can you handle Midnight? He's our fastest horse."

"Yes." Conor's face was pale yet determined. His eyes narrowed. "And afterward, I'll go to the sheriff so we can pull together a posse to find whoever did this."

Seamus nodded. "Be careful."

"I'll be back." He paused in the doorway. "And I'll be praying, Brother," he said as he rushed out the door.

"As will I." Seamus cradled his wife's limp body. "Thank You, Father, that Madeline is still alive. Please heal her. Bring her back to us.

To me. Thank You that the kids weren't here. That they are safe with their friends. Forgive me for leaving her alone. I should have been here."

He fell silent and brushed a strand of hair from her forehead. There were no broken bones, but her bruising and the ripped dress suggested a worse fate. Had the assailant had his way with her? "Please, God, no."

His thoughts went to his brother who hadn't fallen apart at the sight of her blood. Instead, Conor had been cool and firm, taking the initiative to seek out the law. Madeline had changed them all for the better.

Especially himself. Watching her selflessness made him want to be a better man. She thought of others before herself, and nothing was too much trouble. Smart, she'd learned the tasks required to run the household and the farm. Not as fast as she would have liked but sooner than he had upon his arrival. And her patience seemed never-ending, no matter what the kids did.

Visions surfaced of her nibbling her lower lip as she bent over her sewing or the ironing board. Flour smeared on her cheeks while she made bread or biscuits. Smudges of dirt on her forehead while gardening. Eyes sparkling with wit and humor at the dinner table or when seated in the rocker while he read aloud. Her shapely form visible through her cotton dress when outside in the sunshine hanging clothes on the line, her grace evident in the gentle sway of her hips.

"Madeline, can you hear me? Please, wake up." His throat thick, Seamus swallowed. "I'm sorry I wasn't here. You must have been frightened. I won't let anything like this happen again. I won't let you out of my sight."

She moaned, and her eyelids fluttered, but they remained closed.

"Rest easy, my love. Don't try to move. The doctor is coming, but it might be awhile." He nestled her hand in his, rubbing circles with his thumb. Her skin was soft under his touch. Delicate.

Seamus cast his gaze at the ceiling. "I know better than to bargain with You, Lord, but we've suffered a lot of loss as a family. I'd rather not lose Madeline before we've had a chance to cherish the relationship You've granted us, but I give her to You, to do with her as You wish. Certainly, heaven is a better place, but I'd be grateful it if You weren't ready for her yet."

Distant hoofbeats approached, and his heart jumped. He extricated her head from his lap, then jumped to his feet and went to the door. Long hair streaming, Doc Abbott bent low over the neck of his lathered horse. Snorting, the animal thundered down the dirt lane, his sides heaving. Moments later, the doctor reined in the horse and slid to the ground. He wrapped the straps over the railing and vaulted onto the porch. "Where is she?"

"On the floor behind the couch. I was afraid to move her."

"Good because you could have done more damage if you had."

They hurried inside, and the doctor knelt beside Madeline. He looked up at Seamus. "Did she regain consciousness at any time?"

"No."

A shadow crossed Doc Abbott's face. "All right. Well, give me some privacy to examine her, and we'll take it from there."

"Is she going to be okay, Doc?"

"It's too soon to tell, but if you're a praying man, I suggest you do so."

Chapter Twenty-Two

Outside the house, Seamus paced on the porch, his boots clomping against the wood. His chest tight, he wrapped his arms around his middle. He'd been concerned before the doctor's arrival, and the man hadn't given him much hope, making his anxiety soar. Why would Doc Abbott do that? Weren't physicians supposed to make people feel better, especially those waiting for good news?

Head bowed, he prayed, "It's me again, Lord. I know You've already forgiven me, but I want to apologize for my selfishness. I pushed You out of the way so I could be in charge. And we see how well that worked out, didn't we? Thank You for blessing us with Madeline, even if for only this short while. Be with the kids, and help them get over their sadness if she leaves us. If You do heal her, help me to be the best husband a woman could ever want. To put her needs above mine and to lead her in Your ways." A lump formed in this throat. "You can do whatever You wish in this situation, but I ask You to hear my prayer and bring her back to us."

He stood in place, soaking in the warm blanket of peace that had fallen over him. Whatever happened, he would try to accept the outcome.

A hard lesson to learn if it meant the loss of his wife, a woman he hadn't yet told how he felt.

A light breeze fluttered his hair and stroked his cheeks. The familiar smells of cattle and horses, hay and manure, and overturned dirt wafted on the wind. He loved this land even with its difficulties. Was farm life too hard for Madeline? Should he give up the farm for the good of the family? Should he take a job that would provide a regular paycheck? He stuffed his hands into his pockets. He'd be miserable, but perhaps that would be for the best.

Leaning against the porch post, he stared across the rolling landscape, swaths of chocolate-brown soil in the crop fields contrasting with the animals' green pastures. The tips of the tree branches glowed with new life after being dormant all winter. In the corral, Buttercup snuffled at him from near the fence. "Are you calling to me, girl?" He walked to the enclosure, and the mare bobbed her head as if in greeting.

"I don't have anything for you." He rubbed her nose and looked into her intelligent eyes. "Madeline's been hurt, Buttercup, and I won't lie, I'm real worried."

The horse nuzzled his hand and nickered.

"Do you understand me?" He patted her neck. "I'm not sure how much longer I can wait without barging into the house."

Behind him, the door opened, and Seamus whirled. "Doc?" He ran to the cabin and leapt onto the porch with a thud.

Rolling down his sleeves, the doctor shrugged. "I've done all I can for your wife. The laceration on her head was quite nasty, and I had to stitch it. The good news is that there is an outward bump. Otherwise, the swelling might have gone into her brain and caused problems. I'm not saying there hasn't been some of that but probably less than there would have been. I don't think any bones were fractured, but I'll know more when the inflammation goes down."

They went inside. Madeline now lay on the couch, a light blanket on top of her. The bruise was dark against her pale cheek. Seamus's stomach hollowed. "She's still unconscious?"

"Yes. But that may be her body's way of healing itself. Not necessarily a bad thing. Talk to her. Tell her pleasant things. Some doctors have theorized that patients in this condition can hear what's going on. I'm not sure if I hold much stock in the idea, but it doesn't hurt." Dr. Abbott squeezed his shoulder. "Other than her head, there appears to be no other injuries, and in case you're wondering, she wasn't violated."

Seamus's breath came out in a gasp. "Thank You, Jesus."

"Amen." He put on his coat and picked up his bag. "I'll be back to check on her in a couple of days, but if she worsens, send Conor for me."

"Yes, sir. Thank you for coming."

"Anytime, son." With a wave, the doctor left the house. Seconds later, the hoofbeats faded.

Seamus carried a ladder-back chair next to the sofa and sat. He leaned forward, cradling her hands in his. "I'm supposed to talk to you,

Madeline, but I'm not sure what to say." His face flamed. "Well, I do, but I'm afraid to voice what I'm thinking. What if you don't feel the same? I'm not sure I could bear it. I want to tell you how much I love you."

Madeline sighed, and her eyelids fluttered, opening for a moment, then closing.

His heart skittered. "Madeline? Honey, can you hear me?"

She moaned and struggled against the couch, her head moving back and forth.

He laid his hand on her forehead. "It's okay, Madeline. I'm here. You're safe."

Her eyes opened, clouded at first, then clearing. She tried to sit up, then winced and fell against the pillow. "What—?"

"We're not sure what happened, but it looks like someone came in and attacked you. Do you remember anything?"

"You came for me."

"No, you've been in the cabin the whole time. Where do you think you were?"

She put a trembling hand to the side of her skull. "Wasn't I kidnapped?" She shuddered. "I remember the man. He came into the house and chased me around the kitchen. I was able to keep the table between us, but then I thought if I offered him food, he'd take it and leave. He decided he didn't want to eat." Her lips trembled. "He—"

"Take your time, and you don't have to say anything if you don't want."

Nodding, she licked her lips. "So thirsty."

He jumped up, found a glass, and pumped water into it with water. He hurried to her and lifted the glass to her mouth.

Madeline took several sips, then turned her head. "Better. Thank you." She cleared her throat. "He tried to grab me and tore my dress. Then I stumbled and that's all I remember."

"You've got a bump on your head; you must have hit it when you fell."

She frowned. "It hurts."

"The doc had to stitch the laceration." Seamus tucked the blanket under her chin. "I can't tell you how glad I am that you've awakened. I was so scared we'd lost you...that I'd lost you. But, praise God, it seems as if He's going to heal you." He stroked her jaw with the back of his hand. "Does that hurt? How do you feel?"

A crooked smile curved her mouth, then a flash of pain dulled her gaze, and she gasped. "Not well enough to make dinner."

"You're to say on the couch or in bed for the next three days. Doctor's orders. But I might make you rest longer. We don't want you up too quickly." He tucked an auburn tress behind her ear. "Don't worry about a thing. Conor, the kids, and I will split the chores. Or maybe I'll hire someone from town. Doesn't matter. I'll figure it out, but either way, you're to stay—"

Madeline pressed her fingers against his lips. "You're rambling."

With a chuckle, he grabbed her hand, nestling it in his palm. “Truth be told, I’m nervous.”

“Nervous? Whatever for?”

“I had so many things I was going to say to you when you regained consciousness, and now here you are, and I can’t seem to get out the words.”

Another saucy grin, and she cocked her head. “Well, take all the time you need. Apparently, I’m going to be on the sofa for a while.”

He guffawed. “Always the witty one, aren’t you? One of the many things I love about you.” Her eyes widened, and he pushed on. “You heard me correctly. I love you, Madeline Winthrop Fitzpatrick, and shame on me for not telling you sooner. You are the perfect partner in life, and you fill me with joy and laughter. I’m deliriously happy, more so than I’ve ever been.” His heart pounded, and he swallowed. “My only question is whether or not you think you can ever feel the same about me.”

“I already do.” A sheen of moisture shimmered in her eyes, and she smiled, her face glowing. “I’ve been afraid to tell you in case you felt nothing more than fondness for me. I didn’t want to make you uncomfortable.”

Leaning forward, he pressed a soft kiss on her lips. “I’m sorry it took this terrible incident to make me realize how much you mean to me.”

“You call that a kiss?”

“You’re injured. I didn’t want to risk hurting you.”

"A risk I'm willing to take." She snaked her arms around his neck and pulled him toward her, then met his lips with hers, warm, inviting, and full of promise.

Epilogue

The sun had not been long over the horizon when the twins raced out of their bedroom toward the Christmas tree, shrieks of delight filling the cabin. Madeline smiled and rested her hand on her swollen belly. Movement fluttered under her fingers, and her smile broadened. Only a few more weeks, and there would be a new member of the family. Or two. The doctor had hinted that her size suggested she be prepared for two squalling babies.

Propped on the couch with her feet up, she watched the children ooh and aah over the pile of gifts, Conor sitting cross-legged on the floor nearby. The harvest had been plentiful, and several bulls were born in early June, the sale of which brought additional income. The extra funds had allowed Seamus to expand the house, giving them more room for their growing family as well as visitors, such as when her sisters would come to visit in the spring.

God had blessed them mightily. She'd suffered no residual effects from her attack, and the assailant had been found and handed over to law enforcement. Investigation had unearthed allegations of other incidents, including the death of one young woman two counties over. Madeline shuddered. How easily it could have been her.

More activity in her midsection, and her skin stretched and her blouse rippled. Her pregnancy was progressing normally, but she would be glad when she could see her feet while standing. Conor continued to heal, finally able to put his demons to rest. He claimed to be happy as things were, but she often prayed that he'd find companionship. She'd miss him and the twins if they moved out, but the man deserved the happiness a wife and children and living at a place of his own.

From her peripheral vision, she watched Seamus, her gentle and handsome husband. Seated at the end of the couch with her legs in his lap, his expression was one of serenity and joy. Firelight flickered on his face, creating a glow enhanced by the sparkle in his green eyes. As if he felt her gaze, he turned toward her and winked. His warm, calloused hands massaged her puffy ankles, sending tingles to her knees. Her toes curled.

"My gorgeous wife. How are you feeling this morning?"

"Like a whale one might see in New England waters. I cannot believe you find me attractive."

"More than any woman I've ever known, and the fact that you are carrying our children makes you even more beautiful." He patted her hip. "I'm sorry you're so uncomfortable, but I'm hopeful that my Christmas gift will provide some ease over next few weeks."

She leaned over to check the stack of wrapped boxes. "Did you buy me a maid? Or perhaps a cook? How about a laundress? I don't think she will fit inside any of those crates."

He chuckled and sent her a wicked grin. "No, which is why the presents are being shipped on the train. Warren from town will be delivering them." He glanced at the clock over the fireplace. "In fact, we shouldn't have much longer to wait."

"What—"

"Hold your horses, Sister." Conor laughed. "You'll find out soon enough."

"You're in on this too?"

Her brother-in-law shrugged. "Brothers don't keep secrets. And I couldn't have thought of a better gift myself."

Hoofbeats pounded in the yard. Madeline's head whipped toward the window, and she craned her neck to peek through the glass in the breaking daylight. A carriage passed her field of vision. A carriage?

She stilled. What if her present wasn't a what but a who? She shot a glance at Seamus.

A triumphant gleam shone in his eyes. "I do believe your gifts have arrived."

Voices sounded, and the door was flung open. Looking every inch the Boston socialites they were, Cecelia and Phoebe stood on the threshold, their husbands behind them. "Merry Christmas, Madeline," they shouted in unison.

A cold draft swirled into the room, and Seamus rose from the couch. "Welcome to our home. I'm Seamus." He gestured to his brother and the twins. "Conor and his children, Kagan and Kathleen."

Tears streamed down Madeline's cheeks. Cecelia and Phoebe were here. Now. Not in the spring. Her heart swelled as her sisters rushed to her, enveloping her in a hug, talking and laughing at the same time, words tumbling over each other. Looking past Phoebe's shoulder, she saw Seamus shake Elias's and Horace's hands, guiding them to the tree and giving her and her sisters time to rejoice in being together.

She met his gaze across the room, a gaze filled with love and contentment. Her husband. The best gift of all.

THE END

What did you think of *A Bride for Seamus?*

Thank you so much for purchasing *A Bride for Seamus*. You could have selected any number of books to read, but you chose this book.

I hope it added encouragement and exhortation to your life. If so, it would be nice if you could share this book with your family and friends by posting to Facebook (www.facebook.com) and/or Twitter (www.twitter.com).

If you enjoyed this book and found some benefit in reading it, I'd appreciate it if you could take some time to post a review on Amazon, Goodreads, BookBub, or other book review site of your choice. Your feedback and support will help me to improve my writing craft for future projects and make this book even better.

Thank you again for your purchase.

Blessings,
Linda Shenton Matchett

Acknowledgments

Although writing a book is a solitary task, it is not a solitary journey. There have been many who have helped and encouraged me along the way.

My parents, Richard and Jean Shenton, who presented me with my first writing tablet and encouraged me to capture my imagination with words. Thanks, Mom and Dad!

Scribes212 – my ACFW online critique group: Valerie Goree, Marcia Lahti, and the late Loretta Boyett (passed on to Glory, but never forgotten). Without your input, my writing would not be nearly as effective.

Eva Marie Everson – my mentor/instructor with Christian Writers' Guild. You took a timid, untrained student and turned her into a writer. Many thanks!

SincNE, and the folks who coordinate the Crimebake Writing Conference. I have attended many writing conferences, but without a doubt, Crimebake is one of the best. The workshops, seminars, panels, critiques, and every tiny aspect are well-executed, professional, and educational.

Special thanks to Hank Phillippi Ryan, Halle Ephron, and Roberta Isleib for your encouragement and spot-on critiques of my work.

Thanks to my Book Brigade who provide information, encouragement, and support.

Paula Proofreader (https://paulaproofreader.wixsite.com/home): I'm so glad I found you! My work is cleaner because of your eagle eye. Any mistakes are completely mine.

A heartfelt thank you to my brothers, Jack Shenton and Douglas Shenton, and my sister, Susan Shenton Greger for being enthusiastic cheerleaders during my writing journey. Your support means more than you'll know.

My husband, Wes, deserves special kudos for understanding my need to write. Thank you for creating my writing room – it's perfect, and I'm thankful for it every day. Thank you for your willingness to accept a house that's a bit cluttered, laundry that's not always done, and meals on the go. I love you.

And finally, to God be the glory. I thank Him for giving me the gift of writing and the inspiration to tell stories that shine the light on His goodness and mercy.

Next in the Proxy Bride series!

A Bride for Boss by Marisa Masterson

This miracle child is not Frankie's, so why does she risk her marriage her in order to keep the little girl? Frankie's worry is only about her proxy groom. She has no idea of the danger that follows the child.

Frances "Frankie" Elder is brutally frank. It's what led to her firing by the school board. The advertisement for a bride/teacher seems heaven sent. The fact that her groom demands a proxy marriage doesn't faze her. She was already sure this would be a business arrangement rather than a real marriage.

On her way from Wisconsin to Wyoming, Frankie stops in Chicago to buy warmer clothing. Instead, she ends up with a child. What's a woman to do? She's longed for a little one. Besides, the girl clings to her, craving love. But will her husband find the girl as irresistible as she does?

Want more romance? Read on for the first chapter of *Dinah's Dilemma (Westward Home and Hearts Mail Order Brides)*.

May 1870
Lincoln, Nebraska

Chapter One

Nathan Childs raced across the field toward his daughter as she toddled with determination toward the fire. How had he managed to let Florence get so far from his side? The three-year-old was fearless, and he knew better than to give her too much freedom. He'd already prevented her from crawling under the fence into the horse pen and trying to climb one of the massive sugar maples that sheltered the food tables at the town's Memorial Day celebration.

Perspiration trickled down his spine, and his shirt clung to his back as the midday sun beat down on his head and glared into his eyes. The morning had dawned unseasonably warm, and the temperatures continued to rise. Summers in Nebraska were known as scorchers, but May was early to be fighting heat and humidity.

"Florence," he shouted as he ran to gain the child's attention, but his voice was swallowed up in the myriad conversations, music, and laughter of Lincoln's citizens. Nebraska's capital had exploded in population over the last eighteen months, and Burlington and Missouri River Railroad's first train was due at the end of June. Sure to bring even more people. Not what he'd envisioned when he moved West after Georgianna's death.

Finally, close enough to grab her, he scooped Florence into his arms and pressed her close to his chest, her small body warm and soft. "What were you thinking, baby girl? Fire is bad. You need to be more careful and stay near me."

"No!" She arched her back and flailed her legs. "Fire is pretty, Daddy." Her face reddened, and she sobbed as if she'd lost her best friend. Tears dampened her cheeks, her blue eyes swimming.

His heart dropped. He hated when she cried. Her sobs made him feel as helpless as a newborn calf. He never knew what to do when she got like this. He hugged her closer and rubbed circles on her back in an effort to calm her.

"Sounds like someone's tired."

Nathan turned and nodded.

His best friend and the town sheriff, Alfred Denard, approached, a wide grin creasing his face below his black Stetson hat. "How about if you take a break and let Livvy watch her for a while. Looks like you both could use a change of scenery."

"Is it that obvious?"

Alfred chuckled as they headed for the cluster of women seated under the trees. "Sometimes I think you'd rather face the Mes Gang or Farrington Brothers than a crying little girl."

Nathan shrugged. "At least when I was chasing outlaws as a Pinkerton, I'd been trained and knew what to expect. Raising Florence is another whole ball of wax. Every day is different, so something I learned yesterday, doesn't necessarily work today." He blew out a deep breath as Florence quieted and tucked her thumb into her mouth. "I love her with my whole being, but maybe I should have let Georgianna's parents take her. I'm failing miserably."

"Do you think living with her grandparents is what's best for her?"

Nearing the blanket where Alfred's wife, Olivia, sat, Nathan paused and grimaced. "I don't know anymore. The thought of having to decide paralyzes me."

Livvy rose and held out her arms, her blonde hair swept into a tight bun at the base of her neck. She smiled, and her face glowed. "Are you going to let me spend time with your sweet little girl, Nathan? I've been aching to hold that child all day."

Florence chortled and reached for the buxom young woman. Nathan transferred his daughter into her waiting embrace, and his arms felt bereft. He shoved his hands into his pockets.

"Can I keep her through dinner, Nathan?" Livvy poked Florence's belly then rubbed noses with the giggling youngster. "We'll have lots of fun together, won't we?"

"You sure that's not too much time, Livvy?"

She shook her head. "Not enough, if you ask me." She jerked her head toward the corrals. "You boys head over to the pens and enjoy yourselves. The roping competitions should be starting soon."

Alfred ran his finger along her jaw then kissed her cheek, a starry-eyed look on his face. Married for three years, he still mooned over his wife, like a besotted schoolboy. Livvy had come from Atlanta as his friend's mail-order bride. Claiming love at first sight, they'd married immediately. "You holler if you need help, honey."

"I'll be fine." She winked at her husband. "Now, scoot."

Nathan pressed his lips together as his heart tugged. It had been too long since anyone looked at him like Livvy gazed at Alfred, but he had enough going on without saddling himself with a wife. He turned toward the festivities.

He couldn't ask for better friends than Alfred and Livvy. Two days after he'd arrived fifteen months ago, they'd shown up at his claim with food and friendship. Between the two of them, they'd arranged for some of the locals to transport his supplies from Omaha then pulled together a cadre of men to help build the house and barn. Livvy kept him fed when he didn't feel like eating in those early days of mourning after Georgianna's death. He'd figured moving to a new location would lessen the hollow feeling in his heart since she'd never lived in Nebraska, but his grief had followed him.

A city girl born and bred, she would have hated life on the plains, but he still missed her presence. Especially in the small things. Rustling up a stack of pancakes or sitting on the front porch watching the sun dip behind the trees, talking about everything and nothing.

The first year in Lincoln had been difficult, but rewarding. The crop had been decent, and he'd put aside some money for the future. Maybe to purchase the adjoining plot. Too soon to do so, but the idea was tempting. This year's wheat had done well and would be ready to harvest in another couple of months.

A stiff gust kicked up dust from the animal enclosures and swirled above the beasts. The acrid smell of manure clung to the breeze as it lifted his hat. Would he ever get used to the constant wind?

"All right, gents, time to see who's the best roper in the Lincoln." Barnard Johnson, a cattle rancher who owned the largest spread outside of town, stood in the center of one of the corrals, thumbs tucked in the waistband of his denim pants. A pair of ivory-handled pistols, Colts, if Nathan wasn't mistaken, hung from an ornate holster around his substantial belly. His boots gleamed.

Alfred jabbed Nathan with a sharp elbow. "You should take a turn. Show up the rest of the boys."

"No, thanks. I want to make friends not enemies."

"This is just a friendly competition."

"I'll pass, but you should take a turn. Confirm why you're the best sheriff in Nebraska."

"Because I can lasso the outlaws?" Alfred's chuckle rumbled in his chest. "Think I'll pass, too."

"Hey, Nathan. Aren't you going to show off those muscles of yours?"

Nathan cringed at the sound of Katrina Wainwright's strident voice that could send dogs and bats running for cover. She'd made her intentions clear at Christmas that he was the man for her despite his protestations to the contrary. Not one to be put off easily, she turned up at his side every chance she got. He squared his shoulders and pivoted on his heel.

Dipping his head in greeting, he forced a smile. "Good afternoon, Miss Wainwright. Are you enjoying today's event?"

Her giggle ended with a snort as she slapped his arm. "Katrina. How many times do I have to remind you to call me by my given name?"

"It wouldn't be proper, Miss Wainwright."

"We're not exactly in a Boston drawing room."

"True—"

"Hey, Katrina, watch this!" From inside the corral, one of Mr. Johnson's cowhands waved his hands over his head.

She turned, and Nathan took the opportunity to escape. Alfred followed close behind him. They strode to the six-foot tables piled with platters of food, grabbed a couple of plates, and chose several delicious-looking items. Nathan frowned. "That was a close one, but I feel bad for sneaking away."

"Don't. You've made it clear you're not interested. And after the incident with Florence when she took the child from the church nursery without your permission, she ought to know you'll never trust her." Alfred held an oatmeal cookie up to his nose and took a deep breath. "I do love my wife's baking." He took a bite and grinned. Shoving the rest of the treat into his mouth, he clapped Nathan on the back as he finished chewing. "I know how you can get rid of her."

Nathan narrowed his eyes. "I'm afraid to ask."

"Don't be. I have the perfect solution. You need a substitute girlfriend, and I know where you can get one."

"No. Before you say anything else, the answer is no. I'm not going to apply for a mail-order bride." Tears pricked the backs of his eyes. "You and Livvy are very happy, but I'm not in the market for a wife, and I don't think I'll ever be." He swallowed against the lump that had formed in his throat.

"I understand your grief. Don't forget I lost my first wife six years ago. But you can find love again. Unfortunately, the ratio of women to men out here isn't good, and your choices in Lincoln are limited." He wiggled his eyebrows. "Unless, you'd like to reconsider Miss Wainwright."

"Absolutely not." Nathan shuddered. "Despite her outward beauty, she's deceitful, and I could never love a woman like that. Florence and I are doing just fine with the two of us."

"Are you so sure about that? Your little girl needs a mother. You're not being fair to Florence. Please think about contacting Milly Crenshaw at the Westward Home and Hearts Matrimonial Agency." He squeezed Nathan's shoulder. "Now, as much as I enjoy time with you, I'm going to sit with my beautiful wife."

Nathan watched him leave, a jaunty air in his step as he threaded his way through the crowd to Livvy. She beamed as he approached then blushed after he bent and whispered something in her ear.

Was Alfred right? Could he find a woman he would love as he had Georgianna? He surveyed the townspeople, his gaze stopping to rest on Katrina. Full figured with a peaches-and-cream complexion, she had ebony-colored hair and deep-brown eyes. A gorgeous woman evidenced by the number of young men crowding around her like a flock of chicks.

But he couldn't get past her subterfuge. Plain and simple, she'd lied then claimed the whole thing was a misunderstanding. Should he try to find an honest woman who would love Florence as her own? Did this Milly Crenshaw have the answer? Surely, anyone she sent couldn't be any worse than Katrina.

Other Titles

Romance

Love's Harvest, Wartime Brides, Book 1

Love's Rescue, Wartime Brides, Book 2

Love's Belief, Wartime Brides, Book 3

Love's Allegiance, Wartime Brides, Book 4

Love Found in Sherwood Forest

A Love Not Forgotten

On the Rails

A Doctor in the House

Spies & Sweethearts, Sisters in Service, Book 1

The Mechanic & the MD, Sisters in Service, Book 2

The Widow & the War Correspondent, Sisters in Service, Book 3

Dinah's Dilemma (Westward Home and Hearts Mail-Order Brides, 10)

Legacy of Love (Keepers of the Light, coming December 2020)

Mystery

Under Fire, Ruth Brown Mystery Series, Book 1

Under Ground, Ruth Brown Mystery Series, Book 2

Under Cover, Ruth Brown Mystery Series, Book 3

Murder of Convenience, Women of Courage, Book 1

Murder at Madison Square Garden, Women of Courage, Book 2

Non-Fiction

WWII Word Find, Volume 1

CPSIA information can be obtained
at www.ICGtesting.com
Printed in the USA
LVHW091500181220
674449LV00015B/1320